BBC
DOCTOR WHO

BBC CHILDREN'S BOOKS

UK | USA | Canada | Ireland | Australia
India | New Zealand | South Africa

BBC Children's Books are published by Puffin Books,
part of the Penguin Random House group of companies
whose addresses can be found at global.penguinrandomhouse.com.

www.penguin.co.uk
www.puffin.co.uk
www.ladybird.co.uk

Penguin
Random House
UK

First published 2016
001

Written by Jonathan Green
Copyright © BBC Worldwide Limited, 2016

BBC, DOCTOR WHO (word marks, logos and devices),
TARDIS, DALEKS, CYBERMAN and K-9 (word marks and devices) are
trademarks of the British Broadcasting Corporation and are used under licence.
BBC logo © BBC, 1996. Doctor Who logo © BBC, 2009

Printed in Great Britain by Clays Ltd, St Ives plc

A CIP catalogue record for this book is available from the British Library

ISBN: 978–1–405–92650–8

All correspondence to:
BBC Children's Books
Penguin Random House Children's
80 Strand, London WC2R 0RL

BBC

DOCTOR WHO

CHOOSE THE FUTURE

NIGHT OF
THE KRAKEN

JONATHAN GREEN

T 15027

PUFFIN

HOW TO USE THIS BOOK

With this *Choose the Future* book, YOU are in control of the Doctor's story from the very first page to the very last. Every decision you make affects his future – the fate of the universe he protects is in your hands!

Read the first entry, choose what the Doctor should do next, then turn to the number of the entry of your choice. The adventure will unfold as you make new decisions and pick new numbers all the way through the story.

If you think you're ready to embark on a dangerous escapade alongside the Doctor – likely to involve the odd alien nemesis, several perilous encounters, plus an awful lot of running – then turn the page to begin . . .

1

With a grinding wheeze the TARDIS materialises and comes to a juddering halt.

'Right,' says the Doctor, straightening the lapels of his jacket and running a hand through his wiry grey hair. 'Let's take a look around, shall we?'

The wooden door of the impossible blue box springs open and the Doctor bounds through it, only to come to an abrupt halt, surprised by a chill wind coming off the ocean. Dusk has fallen and between black clouds the diamond pinpricks of stars can be seen peppering the sky. There is something familiar about the arrangement of the constellations.

'Definitely Earth,' the Doctor says, sniffing the air as he sets off briskly across a blustery heath. 'Late eighteenth century.' He licks a finger and holds it up, testing the breeze. 'Yes. Cornwall, I'd say, just after sunset.'

He looks back over the wind-tugged grasses of the

darkening moors to the incredible contraption that has brought him here.

'So why are we here, old girl?' he asks, turning back to look at the 1960s police box.

Beyond the TARDIS he can see a rugged coastline. A rocky strip of land juts out into the midnight-black sea beyond, and at the end of the headland the Doctor can just make out the silhouette of a lighthouse tower, the lantern at the top unlit.

The drumming of a horse's hooves sounds, and the Doctor turns to look back across the windswept moor, searching for the animal that is galloping towards him. Then he sees it, a dark shadow against the purpling sky. It is a rider on horseback.

'I'm sure there's nothing to worry about,' the Doctor murmurs to himself.

The horse and rider advance upon the Doctor with every

pounding hoof-beat, and he tries to ignore the gallows he has just spotted out of the corner of one eye, a fraying rope swinging from it in the breeze.

If you think the Doctor should stand his ground, go to 20.

If you think he should take cover as best he can, go to 75.

2

A faded sign hangs from a bracket above the inn door, swinging in the wind that whips over the moor. On it is a painting of an island, like something from a pirate's treasure map, and beneath that, in ornate lettering, the word 'Hispaniola'.

Reaching the inn, the Doctor throws himself through the door and skids to a halt inside, silencing the conversations of the patrons.

The Doctor looks about the large, low-ceilinged room, peering through the smoke that fills the bar, which stings his eyes and makes him cough. On the far side of the room a young woman with dark hair and a tired, sad expression stands behind the bar. The rest of the room is taken up with a jumble of chairs and tables occupied by all manner of individuals who have at least one thing in common: they have decided that an evening in here by the fire is far preferable to being out on the moors on a night like this.

'As you were!' the Doctor blusters, throwing a cautious glance at the door behind him, wondering how long it will be before the dead come knocking.

Keeping a weather eye on the new arrival, the inn's customers return to their conversations, their pipes and their pints.

If the Doctor is going to find out what's going on around here, he is going to have to talk to one of the locals.

If you think he should approach the bar and order himself a drink first, go to 54.

If you think he should try to talk to some of the locals straight away, go to 84.

Alternatively, if the Doctor is already in possession of a map, go to 22.

3

The sonic screwdriver emits a high-pitched whine, then there is a loud bang and sparks fly from the rider's wrist. Rather than cry out in pain or annoyance, though, the rider's shoulders slump and his chin drops on to his chest. He remains upright, but he is also entirely motionless.

Warily, the Doctor approaches the rider and, when the man still doesn't react, grabs hold of his hat and throws it aside. What he sees makes him leap backwards again.

The rider is not a human being at all, but a mechanical man – an android.

'Soliton gas, androids . . . Where have I come across that combination before?' the Doctor ponders. 'There must be a Terileptil lurking around here somewhere. But why?'

With a hiss of equalising air pressures, the hatch in the metal wall behind the Doctor opens.

If you think the Doctor should turn and face whatever is coming through the door, go to 97.

If you think he should get away from this place as fast as he can, go to 79.

4

'I'm the Doctor! Last of the Time Lords, defender of the universe, protector of the laws of time. You might have heard of me.'

The man doesn't say anything, and doesn't move a muscle either.

'And if you have then you'll know that your time is up. Tech like this –' the Time Lord indicates the table with a wave of his hand – 'doesn't belong in eighteenth-century Cornwall and neither, I would guess, do you!'

The Doctor pauses and sighs before continuing. 'Whatever it is you're up to has clearly already got out of hand. But today's your lucky day, because helping people is what I do – particularly people who have got themselves in it up to their necks. Anyway, enough about me. It's time you gave me some answers.'

If you think the Doctor should ask 'Who are you?' –

bearing in mind that the man is still pointing a Fengarian

laser blaster at him – go to 21.

If you think he should ask 'Why are you here?' go to 62.

5

'I knew I wasn't imagining it,' the young woman says, her expression furious and her eyes brimming with tears. 'I knew I saw my Jem again after the hangman strung him up and left him to the crows, even though everyone told me I was wrong! I knew I was right the moment you walked in here tonight with that look in your eyes.'

There can be no doubt now; Jem is the hanged man who has been trailing the Doctor across the moors. In a move he hopes will comfort his new human acquaintance, the Doctor takes the barmaid's hands in his. 'Thank you . . . ?'

'Bess. My name's Bess.'

'Thank you, Bess. I'm the Doctor, by the way.'

The young woman leads the Doctor behind the bar and along a cold stone passageway to the back door of the inn. Opening it cautiously, she peers outside.

'The coast is clear,' she says. 'Let's go. We should head for the village – it's called Bosmouth. We haven't a moment to lose!'

'We?' the Doctor echoes.

'Yes,' Bess says with determination, wiping her eyes with the corner of the shawl she has round her shoulders. 'I'm coming with you.'

If you think the Doctor should refuse to let her accompany him, go to 19.

If you think he should agree to let her join him, go to 24.

Turning on his heel, the Doctor sets off across the moor, back towards the blue box, his pace quickening with every step until he is running.

He is only a few strides from the TARDIS when something steps out of the darkness between him and the time machine. The racing clouds move away from the rising moon for a moment, and the moors are bathed in ghostly light. The Doctor starts at the horror he now sees standing before him.

Its skin is grey and peeling, its hair clogged with earth, and its nose is missing altogether. The cadaver is clad in filthy shroud-like rags, while a noose hangs about its scrawny neck, the dangling rope little more than a frayed knot.

'Steady on there!' the Doctor exclaims, stumbling to a halt before the shambling corpse. 'Who ordered the zombie-gram?'

If you think the Doctor should scan the zombie using his
sonic screwdriver, go to 125.
If you think he should turn and run in the opposite direction
as fast as he can, go to 64.

7

'Last time I checked, eighteenth-century Cornish smugglers didn't deal in spaceship parts!' the Doctor announces boldly.

The man spins round, grabbing something from among the clutter of tech as he does so and exposing what it is he has been tinkering with on the table.

'What are you doing, trying to build a sonic beacon out of salvaged alien technology?' the Doctor asks, intrigued and ignoring the Fengarian laser blaster that is now pointing in his direction. 'Is that for the zombies roaming around on the moor, or for something else?'

There is a haunted look in the man's diamond-hard gaze. 'Who exactly do you think you are?' he growls.

'I'm the Doctor,' the Doctor replies, 'and I have a question for you.'

If you think the Doctor should ask, 'Who are you?' go to 21.

If you think he should ask, 'Why are you here?' go to 62.

If you think he should ask, 'How did you come by all this alien tech?' go to 82.

8

The Doctor is only a few strides from the TARDIS when something steps out of the darkness between him and his precious blue box.

The clouds pass away from in front of the rising moon for a moment, and the moors are bathed in monochrome light. The Doctor starts at the horror he sees standing before him.

Its flesh is grey and worm-eaten, its hair is matted with black earth and its teeth are yellow and half are missing. The figure is clad in clothes that are little more than filthy rags, while a noose hangs slack about its neck, the rope frayed and unravelling.

'Whoa!' the Doctor exclaims, stumbling to a halt out of reach of the shambling corpse. 'I wasn't expecting that!'

If you think the Doctor should speak to the shambling corpse, go to 48.

If you think he should turn and run for it, go to 64.

Warily, the Doctor manoeuvres himself into a crouch, being very careful not to accidentally knock over any of the items strewn around him. Keeping low, he creeps towards the open passageway, his eyes on the man, who has his back turned.

The Doctor's pulse is racing, but he makes it to the tunnel without alerting the man's attention – until his jacket flaps against an out-of-place piece of metallic tubing, which crashes to the floor with a resounding clang.

Not waiting to see the man's reaction, the Doctor races off along the passageway as fast as he can – which is pretty fast, given all the practice he's had over the centuries.

Go to 146.

10

'Now, that's what I call either impeccable timing or incredibly bad luck,' the Doctor says, watching the smuggler as intently as he might an adversary like Colony Sarff.

'Well met, Doctor,' Ravenwood replies.

'Still breaking at least half a dozen Shadow Proclamation regulations, are we?'

'Still trying to save the world, are we?'

'Enough of this!' Bess shouts, interrupting the verbal sparring. 'I've two younger brothers and you're worse than them. Now, if I remember rightly, Doctor, we were about to save my world, never mind the rest of it.'

'Yes, but –'

'Your plan needs three people to work. Well, here's that third person.' Bess turns imploring eyes on the tall, ruggedly handsome rogue. 'Will you help us? Please?'

'Seeing as you asked so nicely –' Ravenwood fixes his flinty eyes on Bess, pointedly ignoring the Doctor, a smile curling the corners of his mouth – 'how could I refuse?'

Go to 147.

11

Making it to the sanctuary of the church, the Doctor throws himself inside and slams the door shut behind him.

'Doctor?'

He jumps, hearing the voice crackle from the walkie-talkie in his jacket pocket.

'Ravenwood?'

'Doctor? Where are you?'

'At the church,' the Time Lord explains. 'I ran into some friends of yours, I believe.'

'Oh, them.' The Doctor can detect the guilt in the smuggler's voice, even over the crackling comm. 'I forgot to deactivate them.'

'I know,' the Doctor riles. 'Pretty nifty security cordon, aren't they? Keeping prying eyes from spying on your nefarious activities.'

'The control unit is in the storeroom under the church.'

'Shouldn't that be "crypt"?'

'Trust me, it's a storeroom.'

A few minutes later, the Doctor is standing in the storeroom, surrounded by all kinds of alien junk and staring at the molecular fringe animation unit.

He is about to deactivate it when an idea strikes him. To defeat the Kraa'Kn spawn would take an army, but that's exactly what is out there stalking the moors – an army of the undead.

If you think the Doctor should try to use the control unit to turn the zombies against the squid-men, go to 122.

If you think he should just stick to the plan, go to 26.

12

It doesn't take the two men long to reach the village. As they hurry along the cobbled street that runs down to the harbour, they quickly realise something terrible has washed in from the sea. Voices raised in panic and ear-splitting screams lead them to the quay, where the people of Bosmouth are desperately trying to defend themselves against attack.

Dozens of creatures, half humanoid and half squid, have emerged from the ink-black waters of the bay within which the village sits, and are advancing on the villagers, tentacles writhing around beak-like mouths, webbed and clawed hands grasping for the terrified humans.

The Doctor watches, appalled, as a fisherman falls under a savage strike from one of the creatures, while a woman runs screaming from the grasping sucker-lined tentacles of another.

'Kraa'Kn!' the Doctor hisses. He turns to the smuggler.

Before he can say anything else, the smuggler says, 'I know.

It's my fault. I'm the reason they're here. I intend to fix things right now.' He points his gun at the Doctor's head.

'What do you think you're doing?' the Doctor yells.

'Duck,' growls the smuggler.

The Doctor does so and the gun fires. An octopus-headed creature drops to the cobbles behind the Doctor and lies twitching for a moment before falling still.

'There was no need for that!' the Doctor exclaims.

'Don't mention it,' mutters the smuggler.

'No more killing!' commands the Doctor.

'I thought you wanted me to clean up my mess!'

'Not like this.'

'How then?'

A shrill scream suddenly cuts through the night.

If the Doctor has met Bess the barmaid, go to 81.

If not, go to 91.

13

The sound of the smuggler's footsteps on the shingle mask the approach of another person across the beach. As the man prepares to pull the trigger of the laser blaster, Bess swings the piece of driftwood she is carrying like a club, hitting him over the back of the head and knocking him to the ground.

He lands face first in the wet sand and doesn't move.

'Have I killed him?' the young woman asks, her face ashen, as the Doctor feels for a pulse.

'No. He'll live to smuggle another day,' the Doctor reassures her.

Bess sighs, a look of relief washing over her face.

'Thanks for the help.' The Doctor picks up the man's gun and hurls it as far out to sea as he can. It lands with a splash and he sees a churning in the water a little further away. 'Now, more importantly, what is that?'

'What is what?' Bess asks, turning to see what has caught the Doctor's attention.

'That movement in the water,' he replies. 'Can't see well enough from here. Need a better vantage point.'

'How about the village? Or over there?' Bess asks, pointing to the lighthouse.

If you think the Doctor should go to the village, go to 37.

If you think he should go to the lighthouse, go to 67.

14

'You would dare to threaten me?' the Doctor exclaims in irritated disbelief. 'You don't threaten me unless you've got an entire Cyber-fleet, a Dalek attack force and a Sontaran battle group to back you up, and even then I would advise against it.'

The Doctor breaks off suddenly. A flutter of movement in the corner of his eye has caught his attention, sending shivers down his spine as he becomes aware of the presence of something behind him.

He turns slowly and comes face-to-face with a vision straight out of a nightmare.

Standing before him is a thing that was once a man. Its flesh is grey, its hair matted with grave-dirt, and its nose is missing entirely. The corpse-like figure lunges for the Doctor with a speed he wouldn't have expected and he finds himself in its bony grip, a grip that is as strong as a steel trap.

'What is this?' the Time Lord challenges the rider. 'You find making friends so hard you have to go digging them up?'

The next thing the Doctor feels is a sharp blow to the back of the head, and then nothing more.

Go to 59.

15

'There's a shadow over Bosmouth,' the Doctor explains, 'and we need to shed some light on the situation if we're going to clear up this mess – catch my drift?'

Bess looks to the lighthouse, her own face lighting up with sudden understanding.

'The lighthouse, of course! But how will that stop the Kraa'Kn?'

'You'll see.' The Doctor grins. 'Remember what Billy Ocean said to do when the going gets tough?'

'William Ocean? Is he a famous naval officer?'

'Never mind, wrong time period,' says the Doctor. 'Now, come with me if you want to live!'

Go to 67.

16

The Doctor does his best to keep up, taking bounding strides over the grassy moor, but he soon loses sight of the rider when the man turns off the road, steering his horse towards the isolated church.

'At least I know where you're going,' the Doctor gasps breathlessly, making for the church too. The horse and rider have blended in with the shadows and disappeared from view.

As the Doctor approaches the graveyard wall, he hears the rustling of paper on the breeze and catches sight of a piece of parchment fluttering over the grass nearby.

If you think the Doctor should chase after the fleeing piece of parchment, go to 43.

If you think he should ignore it, go to 86.

'What can I get you?' the young woman asks as the Doctor approaches the bar.

'How about a nice cup of tea?'

'You can have ale or water,' the barmaid tells him bluntly.

'One glass of water then, please.'

The woman plonks a tankard down on the bar. The Doctor picks it up and peers at the dirty-looking liquid inside. He puts it back down on the bar, deciding he's not thirsty after all.

'So, nice weather we're having for the time of . . . year,' the Doctor remarks awkwardly.

'Weather's the least of our worries,' the barmaid replies.

If you think the Doctor should ask her about the gallows he saw on the moor, go to 89.

If you want him to ask her about the mysterious rider, go to 47.

If you want him to find out about the lighthouse, go to 69.

18

'What is it?' he asks, joining her by the glass.

'The ship – the wreck, I mean,' says Bess, pointing. 'It looks so tiny from up here.'

'It's just a matter of perspective,' he replies, turning back to the jumble of technology strewn about the tower. He suddenly whirls round again, exclaiming, 'It's just a matter of perspective!'

'Are you all right, Doctor?' Bess says, startled.

'I have a plan,' he says, eyebrows raised and a grin on his face, which a moment later is replaced by an intense scowl. 'But we'll really need three people for it to work.'

Both Bess and the Doctor jump as they hear a creak on the stairs and a cloaked figure enters the lantern room.

If the name Ravenwood means anything to the Doctor, go to 10.

If not, go to 135.

19

'I'd really rather you didn't.' The Doctor sighs. 'I'd prefer not to have your well-being on my conscience. I appreciate you helping me out, but the best thing you can do right now is stay inside. Lock the doors and don't let anyone in or out until I return. Okay?'

'Very well,' Bess says reluctantly, her expression downcast.

'Right you are then. Now go and make yourself a hot chocolate and curl up by the fire. I have a feeling it's going to be a long night.'

'Hot chocolate?' the girl says, laughing. 'You mean like they have in those fine chocolate houses up in London?'

'If you like,' the Doctor replies. 'But remember, no one comes or goes without my say-so.'

And then he is striding off across the moors again, ears straining for the sound of shuffling footsteps and moaning voices. But where is he headed?

If you think the Doctor should go to the village of Bosmouth, go to 96.

If you think he should take the coastal cliff path, go to 131.

20

'Hello!' the Doctor calls, waving at the approaching horseman.

Seeing the Doctor, the rider pulls on the reins, bringing his horse to a halt still some distance away.

He is dressed head to toe in black, from the hat on his head down to his long riding boots. His stallion is also black, except for a white flash on its nose. The last light of day is fading, and the Doctor observes that the stranger keeps his face in the shadows as if to hide it.

'Who goes there?' The rider shouts his challenge, raising a flintlock pistol menacingly before him.

'Just a traveller, lost on the moors this blustery night,' the Doctor says.

'And do you have a name, sir?'

'I'm the Doctor,' the Doctor says, holding out a hand and taking a step towards the horse.

'Stay back!' the rider barks. 'Lost, are you?' He indicates the shadowy silhouette of the TARDIS. 'Is that anything to do with you? Because it wasn't here earlier.'

'I didn't catch your name,' the Doctor says, taking another step towards the man.

'I said stay back!' the man snaps, pointing his gun directly at the Doctor.

If you think the Doctor should run for cover, go to 56.

If you think he should try to keep the rider talking, go to 40.

21

For a moment the stranger simply keeps his steely gaze fixed on the Doctor. Then his shoulders sag, the tension appears to leave his body, and – most importantly – he lowers the gun in his hand.

'You can call me Ravenwood,' the man says.

'Oh, I see,' replies the Doctor. 'A false name. Well, Mr Ravenwood, you can simply call me Doctor.'

'And I suppose Doctor is the name you were born with, is it?' Ravenwood says.

'Names aren't important,' mutters the Doctor.

'I would beg to differ,' counters Ravenwood. 'Especially your name, Doctor. You see, I've heard rumours whispered as far away as the Maldovarium of the one known as the Doctor. If you're who you say you are, then I must concede I could actually use your help.'

A plea for help?

Just moments ago Ravenwood was pointing a Fengarian laser blaster at the Doctor, and that recollection alone makes the Time Lord reluctant to help now.

If you think the Doctor should agree to help Ravenwood anyway, go to 112.

If you think he should refuse to help the man, go to 42.

22

Something about the layout of the room reminds the Doctor of the map he has tucked away in his jacket. Taking it out, he looks from the crude outlines on the parchment to the room and back again.

Once he has everything in alignment, he focuses his attention on the spot marked by the X. The simplistic drawing of a fireplace clearly lines up with the nook in the wall, and the X is positioned over one corner of it.

Ignoring the bewildered stares of the locals, the Doctor makes his way over to the fireplace and peers at the sooty bricks, trying to work out what the map could refer to.

Then he sees it.

The mortar has been removed from around one of the bricks in the corner. Tugging on it, the Doctor discovers the brick is loose. He removes it with one hand, then reaches cautiously into the hole with the other and pulls out a large iron key.

'Curiouser and curiouser,' says the Time Lord, as he pops the key into his pocket.

If you think the Doctor should now try talking to some of the locals, go to 84.

If you think it best that he leaves the Hispaniola Inn, go to 107.

23

As the Doctor flees for his life over the moor, he catches sight of another isolated building. This one is unmistakably a church, with its tower and surrounding wall.

The building on the crest of the hill, on the other hand, glows like a beacon offering weary travellers sanctuary from the elements and the darkness. It must be a coaching inn.

But which building will offer the Doctor the greatest protection from the pistol-toting rider?

If you think the Doctor should head towards the church, which is the nearer of the two buildings, go to 116.

If you think he should keep running towards the inn, go to 98.

24

'I may not be much of a people person, but I am quite accustomed to having company when I'm about to face certain danger,' says the Doctor.

He and Bess leave the inn, unnoticed by either the clientele or the pack of zombies waiting for him on the other side of the building.

'After all,' he adds. 'Where's the fun in adventure if you haven't got someone to share it with?'

He glances over his shoulder at the girl, who is having to jog to keep up with his long strides.

'So, Bess the barmaid, where do you suggest we go now?'

'The village?' Bess offers. 'Or perhaps the lighthouse?'

If you think they should go to the village, go to 37.

If you think they should go to the lighthouse, go to 67.

25

'Ladies and gents!' the Doctor shouts over the noise, leaping on to a table in the middle of the room. 'If I might have your attention please!'

At once all eyes are on him and the anxious chattering subsides to a confused murmur.

'Good people of Cornwall, we are under attack. This night the dead have risen to besiege the living!'

'What can have done this?' A voice comes from the crowd. 'An evil spirit? Witchcraft?'

'Probably,' the Doctor says. 'But that's not important. What's important are your families. Your loved ones. Where are they right now?'

'The village!' someone gasps.

'Precisely. And who's going to save them if not you?'

'But what can we do?' This time a dissenting voice escapes from the huddle.

'Alone, nothing. But together what *can't* we do?'

The excited hubbub returns, but with an edge of confidence now.

'To Bosmouth!' shouts a bald, burly man. He throws open the door of the inn and leads the incensed mob out into the night.

If you think the Doctor should go with them, go to 38.

If you think he should join the barmaid at the back of the room, go to 5.

26

'No! Now's not the time to get distracted,' he chides himself. 'I need to remain focused and deal with Kroll the Second out there in the bay.'

The Doctor deactivates the molecular fringe animation unit, and the humming of the device fades into silence.

Leaving the storeroom, he makes his way back through the church and opens the door to the outside world, to discover that he is alone once more.

'Thank goodness for that!' he declares, before setting off again at a run.

Go to 35.

27

Making for the main exit behind the advancing pack of zombies is a bold move and also, as it turns out, a futile one.

The shambling corpses quickly surround the Doctor, despite their ungainly movements, and he finds himself trapped at the centre of a steadily closing circle of the undead.

'I don't suppose I could appeal to your better natures?' the Doctor tries, but the zombies do not even falter in their advance.

They claw at him with fingernails black with grave-dirt, and the Doctor realises that there is no escaping his fate now.

He feels a sharp blow to the back of his head and blacks out.

Go to 59.

28

As far as the Doctor can recall, Cornishmen in this era weren't renowned for having access to futuristic alien technology – but that is precisely what he sees lying on the makeshift table. There is part of a Sontaran cloaking device, what looks like a Vintaric crystal matrix from a Terileptil ship, and something organic-looking, which he suspects is Zygon in origin.

Interestingly, the man now appears to be engrossed in constructing or trying to repair something on the table in front of him.

If you think the Doctor should leave now, while the man is distracted, go to 9.

If you think he should challenge the man, go to 7.

29

'Because I'm the Doctor and I help people, aliens, digital-viral life forms – take your pick.'

'You said that you have encountered my people before,' the Terileptil says, its interest clearly piqued. 'Was that on this world too?'

'Yes,' the Time Lord says warily. 'But it didn't end well.'

'What do you mean, Doctor?'

'The Grim Reaper, plague, fire, half of seventeenth-century London wiped out. You know how it is.' He gives a dismissive wave of his hand. 'But tell me, what brings you here?'

'My craft crashed on this world. In its damaged state, the ship automatically activated the hibernation protocols designed to keep the crew alive until help can arrive.'

As the alien speaks, gill flaps on the side of its head open and close independently of its speech patterns as it inhales the soliton-rich air.

'But the awaited rescue did not come,' it continues. 'So I remained here, trapped for centuries. In the interim, a temple was raised over the place where my ship lay buried. I was only awakened from my stasis-sleep when the humans came – smugglers looking for somewhere to hide their wares.'

'So why the android disguised as one of the humans?' the Doctor asks, intrigued now.

A low hiss escapes from between the Terileptil's fish-like teeth. 'Why should I answer any more of your questions, Doctor, when what you have already told me implies that we should be anything but allies? That you are, in fact, the enemy of the Terileptils?'

'Now hang on. That was a long story cut very sho–'

The Doctor's self-defence comes to an abrupt end as another bolt of intense purple energy pierces the murky atmosphere aboard the Terileptil ship and strikes him in the chest.

With an exhalation of shock, the Doctor drops to the floor unconscious.

Go to 126.

30

'Are you going to tell me your name?' hisses the Doctor. 'And perhaps what you want?'

'You can call me Ravenwood,' the man replies, 'and what I need, Doctor, is your help.'

'How did you figure that out?' the Time Lord asks.

'I've been watching you, following you. I've seen your work. You're the Doctor and you help people. Will you help me?'

'I assume this –' the Doctor indicates the lighthouse and the seething sea below with a wave of his hand – 'is something to do with you?'

'Yes,' the man confesses, looking down at the ground, unable to hold the Doctor's gaze.

'Then no, I won't help you,' the Time Lord states coldly. 'I'm not in the habit of helping people who make demands at gunpoint. But I will help the people of that village down there, if I can. And, seeing as you're not from round these parts yourself, you might just have what I'm after to help them in their hour of need.'

The man nods. 'We must end this tonight. One way or another.'

Go to 53.

31

'Are you sure about that?' the Doctor asks, taking off across the beach.

He hears the blaster fire behind him and a spout of water and wet sand erupts into the air to his left. Rather than causing the Doctor to think better of running away, it simply spurs him on in his flight from the smuggler.

What he needs is somewhere to shelter – somewhere like the ship grounded due to bad weather on the beach nearby. Or maybe a better idea would be to lose himself among the cobbled alleyways of the cliff-hugging village.

If you think the Doctor should go towards the grounded ship, go to 55.

If you want him to go towards the village, go to 96.

32

The Doctor follows a steep track down the cliff to the beach, grabbing on to clumps of grass to support himself as he descends. Once he is safely down on the sand, he makes his way towards the sea and can't help but be curious about the ship that lies wrecked on the beach.

Out beyond the shoreline, the frothing disturbance in the rolling black waves shows no sign of abating.

If you think the Doctor should explore the wrecked ship, go to 44.

If you think he should investigate the disturbance out in the bay, go to 63.

33

'Who are you and what do you want?' hisses the Doctor, realising that he is talking to the mysterious rider he first encountered on the moors above Bosmouth.

'You can call me Ravenwood,' the man replies, 'and what I need, Doctor, is your help to save the people of the village.'

'How do you know who I am?' the Time Lord snaps irritably. Being fired upon has not put him in the best frame of mind.

'Your reputation precedes you. Besides, I have been watching you. Following you.'

The Doctor eyes the smuggler suspiciously. 'Why?'

'I already told you: because I need your help. Will you help me, Doctor?'

The Time Lord frowns. 'I'm not in the habit of helping those who negotiate at gunpoint, but I will help these people –' he indicates the villagers – 'and the Kraa'Kn too, given half the chance. And, seeing as you're not from round these parts yourself, maybe together we can help them in their hour of need.'

'Then you have to follow me,' Ravenwood implores him. 'We have to reach the lighthouse.'

'So be it. Lead on, Ravenwood.'

Go to 52.

34

The Doctor follows the tunnel round to the left, and then to the right as it turns again, until he emerges into a well-lit underground chamber. Large barrels line the walls, along with a number of wooden crates, some of which have straw spilling from them.

He might have expected to find a burial crypt full of mouldering coffins under the church, but not a storeroom such as this. On the other side of the room, another passageway leads away into darkness.

'Smugglers' tunnels,' the Doctor mutters to himself.

During this period of Earth's history, it was not uncommon for people to bring illegal goods in from abroad via hidden coves and secret tunnels such as these. They wanted to avoid officials at established ports up and down the Cornish coast.

However, as far as the Doctor can recall, Cornish smugglers didn't deal in tech from the future, which is precisely what he can see lying on a makeshift table fashioned from an old door placed across a pair of upended barrels. Standing in front of this table is a man dressed in dark eighteenth-century clothes, his shoulder-length black hair tied in a ponytail.

Hearing the Doctor arrive, the man spins round and grabs something from the table as he does so. He points the device at the Time Lord, who instantly recognises it as a Fengarian laser blaster.

There is an intense, hunted look in the man's flinty gaze. 'Who,' he growls, 'are you?'

If you think the Doctor should reply, 'I am the Doctor!' go to 4.

If you think he should take out his psychic paper and try to fool the man, go to 51.

35

Finally the Doctor reaches the TARDIS and flings himself inside. Running to the central console, he flicks on the monitor and sets to work, his fingers dancing over the controls.

Plugging his bright-yellow plastic walkie-talkie into a socket on the console, the Doctor says, 'Bess, can you hear me?'

'Hello?' The young woman's voice crackles in the air. 'What magic is this? Doctor, can you hear me?'

'Yes, I can hear you. Ravenwood, are you there?'

'Receiving you loud and clear,' answers the smuggler.

'Is the beacon in position?'

'It is.'

The Doctor flicks a series of switches and the time rotor begins to turn.

'Then let's do this!'

The wheezing becomes louder and the TARDIS starts to shake, the Doctor bracing himself against the console.

'Bess, flick the switch!'

High up in the lighthouse, Bess does as she is told.

The light on top of the TARDIS starts to pulse, then it emits a beam of intense blue light, which soars across the moor, striking the lighthouse.

Inside the lantern room, Bess turns away to protect her eyes from the glare of the light hitting the huge mirror. This light is refocused by the pulse cannon, which in turn produces a ray of golden flame, banishing the night over Dead Man's Bay.

Lying flat in the grass at the top of the cliffs, Ravenwood watches as the last of the squid-men stumble inside the wreck of the merchant ship, drawn to the vessel by the sonic beacon and then forced inside to escape the light.

The beam's waveform changes and begins to pulse, and with every pulse something incredible happens: the wreck, and everything contained within it, starts to shrink.

Soon it is no bigger than a dinghy, and then only moments later Ravenwood can't even see it from his vantage point.

Go to 46.

36

'Lovely to see you again!' the Doctor calls as he sprints past the robot. It reaches for him clumsily, as if its joints have started to rust, but it is far too slow – the Doctor is long gone.

The chiselled and chipped rock walls of the tunnel eventually give way to the sea-shaped galleries of a coastal cave. The remnants of broken barrels and boxes lie partially buried in the dark, wet sand, along with coils of tarred rope and glass bottles half full of seawater.

His footsteps rattling on the shingle that has been cast up into the cave by the relentless tides, the Doctor emerges at last on to the shore below the towering granite cliffs. As he stumbles down the beach he peers through the night, taking in the rough seascape before him.

To his left, he can see the twinkling lights of a village that hugs the cliffs surrounding a natural harbour. To his right, at the end of the promontory, is the looming silhouette of the lighthouse, while in front of him is the wreck of a ship washed up on the shore.

Hearing pounding footsteps behind him, the Doctor turns slowly, hands half in the air, already knowing what he will see. And, sure enough, there's the smuggler, the alien blaster held tight in both hands.

'No more running,' he says and takes aim.

If the Doctor has met Bess the barmaid, go to 13.

If not, go to 31.

37

It doesn't take the Doctor and Bess long to reach the village nestled at the foot of the cliffs, but as they run down a cobbled slipway between the brick and timber buildings they realise that something else has got there before them.

Voices raised in panic and shrill screams lead them to the harbour, where the people of Bosmouth are defending their homes. They are not under attack from opportunistic pirates or looters, however, but horrifying monsters from the sea.

Hundreds of squid-like humanoid creatures are emerging from the oily black waters of Dead Man's Bay, in which the village sits, and advancing on the desperate villagers, tentacles writhing around beak-like mouths.

The Doctor and Bess arrive in time to see a man fall to a swipe from a clawed, webbed hand, while a woman is grabbed by sucker-lined tentacles and dragged, screaming, within reach of a snapping beak mouth.

'Kraa'Kn!' the Doctor growls.

'The Kraken?' Bess gasps. 'But I thought the tales were just legend!'

'And where do all legends originate if not from some long-forgotten truth?' the Doctor asks.

'I just don't understand how they can be real!' Bess cries.

'Look, I wish I could tell you this was all some wild imagining, but unfortunately the Kraa'Kn are real. Looks like a mass spawning to me,' the Doctor goes on, 'and the first thing the young will need to do is feed.'

'The young?' Bess stares in shock at the six-foot-tall squid-men rising from the harbour. 'If they're the young, then I'd hate to meet their mother.'

'Trust me,' the Doctor says, a wild gleam in his eye, 'you would.'

Turning on his heel, he hurries back up the slipway, away from the harbour.

'Wait! Where are you going? We can't just leave. We have to help.'

'I agree,' the Doctor calls back.

'Well I'm staying here!' Bess yells.

If you think the Doctor should insist that Bess goes with him, go to 57.

If you think he should leave her behind and carry on alone, go to 131.

38

Ignoring the biting cold of the harsh wind now howling over the moors, the Doctor follows the enraged mob out of the inn and into the advancing zombie horde.

'Once more unto the breach!' the Doctor shouts, rallying his improvised troops.

There are more of the zombies than ever before. Surveying the scene of battling Cornishmen and clawing corpses, the Doctor recognises all the signs of molecular fringe animation. Someone is employing alien technology to harness the dead to her, his or its will. But who, and why?

What's certain is that the Doctor won't find answers if he doesn't take action.

If you think the Doctor should lead the mob towards the village of Bosmouth, go to 50.

If you think he should leave the mob and head towards the lighthouse along the coast, go to 131.

39

'Did you say something?' the Doctor calls to Bess, a frown creasing his features. 'Saving the world is distracting me a little!'

Using the solar pulse cannon, a Fengarian power cell and the guts of a Sontaran teleport unit, the Doctor cobbles together a contraption while Bess, who has come to join him, looks on worriedly.

'What is it?' she asks, as the Doctor lines the cannon up with the mirror of the lighthouse lantern, then angles the barrel so that it is pointing at the bay far below.

'It's now or never,' the Doctor replies. 'And I've always been much more of a now person, no matter when now actually is. The question is, who do I save? The humans or the Kraa'Kn?'

If you think the Doctor should save the Kraa'Kn, go to 58.

If you think he should save the people of Bosmouth, go to 138.

40

'Now, now, there's no need for that,' the Doctor says in as casual a manner as he can manage – which is really quite casual, due to the countless times he's found himself at the wrong end of a gun. 'I was merely making what I believe is called small talk, one traveller to another.'

'You won't catch me out that way,' the rider says, his eyes darting from the Doctor to the TARDIS and back again. 'And if you think you're taking me anywhere in that –' he glances back at the blue box – 'you've got another thought coming.'

'Take you where? What are you talking about?'

'Very clever,' the rider says with a smile that doesn't reach as far as his eyes. 'But, like I said, you're not going to catch me out so easily. You're too late anyway.'

'Too late? What are you on about now?' the Doctor demands, becoming increasingly irritable in the face of hostility. 'Listen, this paranoia thing isn't doing you any favours. It's very unbecoming.'

'Walk away,' the rider says, his voice a low growl. 'That would be my advice to you. Walk away, leave this place and never look back, if you know what's good for you.'

If you think the Doctor should take the stranger's advice and leave while he still can, go to 6.

If you think he shouldn't risk turning his back on the stranger, go to 14.

41

The Doctor eyes the strange assortment of metallic objects covering the makeshift table.

'Last time I checked, Cornish smugglers didn't deal in alien technology!' the Doctor announces boldly, springing to his feet.

The man spins round in surprise, grabbing something from the table as he does so. He points the device at the Time Lord, who instantly recognises it.

'Ha! A Fengarian laser blaster!' the Doctor exclaims.

There is an intense, hunted look in the man's flinty gaze. He looks very unfriendly.

If you think the Doctor should say, 'I am the Doctor!' go to 4.

If you think he should take out his psychic paper and try to dupe the smuggler, go to 77.

42

'You really think I'm going to help you after you were prepared to shoot me at virtually point-blank range with that?' the Doctor fumes, pointing at the Fengarian laser blaster still gripped tightly in the man's hand.

'So you don't like me waving a laser blaster at you,' Ravenwood replies. 'Very well.'

Go to 108.

The Doctor bounds after the wind-propelled parchment and plucks it from the air just before another gust would have sent it dancing across the heath.

Peering at it he sees, thanks to what little moonlight is escaping the cloud cover overhead, that it is a map drawn in unsteady lines of black ink.

'Looks like the floor plan of a building,' the Doctor murmurs, turning the map through ninety degrees. 'But which building? And what spot is this X supposed to mark, if this bit is a fireplace?' He jabs a finger at the piece of paper, recognising the shape of a chimney breast on the plan.

He finds his gaze drawn to the horizon and the low building on the ridge of the hill, just as a cloud obscures the face of the moon.

Tucking the map inside his jacket, he continues on his way.

Go to 130.

44

Now that he is up close, the Doctor can see that a huge hole has been torn in the side of the ship. But what could have ripped up nailed planks of tarred wood? Was it a submerged reef, or something else?

Cautiously he makes his way inside through the hole in the hull, and finds himself in the cargo hold of the vessel. It would appear that whatever cargo the ship was carrying has either been lost to the sea or been stolen by locals when it first ran aground a couple of nights ago.

But the ship is not entirely empty. Hearing a sucking, slurping sound, the Doctor spins round and comes face-to-face with a horrifying vision that is half octopus and half man.

The creature moves towards the Doctor from the gloomy interior of the hull, reaching for him with fingers that look like squirming slugs. Its skin glistens green-grey, like that of some deep-sea monster. Although its body is humanoid, its head looks like that of a squid, complete with writhing tentacles.

The Doctor can't help but give a cry of alarm at what he sees.

'Kraa'Kn! Primitive, vicious and usually hungry!'

Then he is sprinting out of the wreck and back on to the beach in an effort to escape the clutches of the squid-man.

Go to 76.

45

Deciding that it's time to leave the inn and continue his investigations elsewhere, the Doctor pulls the collar of his jacket up against the wind and opens the door. He immediately shuts it again when he sees what is waiting for him outside – a whole pack of decomposing corpses, their skeletal hands outstretched, ready to seize him.

'Hey! Look out there!' comes a voice.

People crowd around the leaded windows and peer out into the night, seeing for themselves what the Doctor has already witnessed.

If he is going to find out what's going on along this isolated stretch of Cornish coast, or even just get back to the TARDIS, the Doctor is going to have to face the zombie pack waiting outside. Then he sees the barmaid beckoning to him, mouthing the words, 'Out the back!'

If you think the Doctor should follow the barmaid, go to 5.

If you think he should try to rally the people to help him deal with the undead mob, go to 25.

46

'Thanks for this,' the Doctor says later, holding a large glass bottle in front of his face and peering at the wreck contained within. Its tattered sails flap in an impossible breeze while tiny octopus-headed figures can be seen through the rift in its side, moving around inside the hull.

'It was the least I could do,' says the smuggler.

'Yes, it was,' the Doctor points out.

'It's a ship in a bottle,' Bess says, laughing with wonder.

'How did you do it?' asks Ravenwood.

'It's similar to the matter-conversion technology utilised by the Daemons, but with a dash of Gallifreyan dimensional mathematics thrown in, to maintain the size–weight ratio. You could say it's bigger –'

'It's smaller on the outside!' Bess marvels.

'Yes, if you like.' The Doctor sighs, the wind having been taken out of his sails.

The sun is rising beyond the rooftops of Bosmouth on the other side of the bay, shining with a gleaming golden light. The beach is empty now apart from the TARDIS standing on the wet sand, casting a long shadow behind it.

'So what happens now?' Ravenwood asks.

'I'll take this with me,' the Doctor says, turning the bottle about in his hands, 'and find some quiet backwater world and release the Kraa'Kn back into the wild. What about you?' the Doctor asks the smuggler. 'Am I going to have to keep an eye on you?'

'You don't need to worry about me,' Ravenwood says, looking at Bess rather than the Doctor. 'I think I might hang around here for a while.'

The Doctor rolls his eyes. 'Humans! So this is farewell then.'

Ravenwood offers the Doctor his hand. 'Farewell, Doctor.'

Go to 120.

47

'Could have been a smuggler,' the barmaid replies, when the Doctor asks her about the mysterious rider he saw on the moors. 'Smuggling goes on all up and down the coast. Rogues not keen on paying King George's taxes and hoping to avoid getting caught.'

'Smuggling, eh?'

The young woman leans forward across the bar and adds in a whisper, 'Rumour has it they make use of hidden tunnels under the moors.'

'Is that so?'

If you think the Doctor should ask Bess about the lighthouse, go to 69.

If you think he should ask about the gallows, go to 89.

If you think he should talk to someone else, go to 109.

If you think he should leave the inn, go to 107.

48

'Hello! Fancy meeting you here,' the Doctor calls out. 'I say, what lovely weather we're having for the time of century.'

The shambling corpse says nothing; only the foul stench of decomposing lungs escapes its yawning mouth in a rattling exhalation.

'All right then – well, actually, you're clearly not all right. You're a zombie!'

If you think the Doctor should run for it, go to 64.

If you think he should use his sonic screwdriver to scan the zombie, go to 125.

49

Whatever the Terileptil has planned, the Doctor knows that its scheme will conclude at the top of the lighthouse.

Bursting into the tower, he takes the wooden stairs two at a time, emerging into the lantern room at the summit panting for breath.

'Whatever it is you're about to do, don't do it!' shouts the Doctor, taking in the Terileptil, the android – which has now shed its disguise – and the curious device that has somehow been wired into the mechanisms of the lighthouse.

'You would stop me sending a distress signal, Doctor?'

'A distress signal?'

'What else am I supposed to do?' the alien challenges the Time Lord. 'My ship is no longer capable of flight, let alone interstellar travel. Even its life-support systems are barely operational now. My intention is only to call for help from my own kind.'

'And my only concern is which faction might answer your

interstellar call when you phone home,' the Doctor replies. 'The friendly fish-lizard kind or the burn-down-seventeenth-century-London-after-failing-to-exterminate-the-human-race kind.'

'You will not stop me, Doctor!' the Terileptil gurgles and moves to activate the signalling device, as the android advances towards the Time Lord.

The Doctor realises immediately that he can only stop one of them. Which is it to be?

If you think the Doctor should stop the Terileptil, go to 137.

If you think he should stop the android, go to 102.

50

It doesn't take long to reach the village. As he leads the mob down a cobbled street into the heart of Bosmouth, the Doctor hears the echoes of terrified screams and voices raised in panic. Spurred on by the sounds, he and the mob head towards the harbour, where they come upon a shocking scene.

The villagers are engaged in a battle with dozens of nightmare creatures from the deep sea. They stand six feet tall on their hind legs, their semi-humanoid bodies topped with octopus-like heads. Each has a fringe of suckered tentacles, a beak-like mouth and hands that are both webbed and clawed.

Although the creatures do not carry any weapons or wear any armour, they appear to be more than a match for the poor people of Bosmouth.

'Kraa'Kn!' gasps the Doctor.

The party from the inn joins the fight, no longer needing

the Doctor's words to encourage them, and the Doctor looks over to the darkened lighthouse at the top of the cliffs.

'There's a shadow over Bosmouth,' he mutters to himself, 'and we need to shed some light on this miserable situation.'

A single scream cuts through the night, making the Doctor jump.

It is in the Doctor's nature to save people, but should he use precious time helping one person when the entire village is at risk?

If you think the Doctor should head in the direction of the scream, go to 80.

If you think he should head to the lighthouse and put his plan to save the village into action, go to 131.

51

The Doctor whips out the wallet containing the psychic paper and brandishes it in the man's face. Before he can come up with an excuse for his being there, the man exclaims, 'You're a Time Agent working for the Shadow Proclamation? Well, you're not taking me in – dead or alive!' And, with that, he takes aim and fires.

A chunk of brick explodes in the tunnel wall past the Doctor's shoulder.

'Steady on!' the Doctor shouts.

'Focusing crystal must be out of alignment,' the man mutters to himself, and then to the Doctor he says, 'but I won't miss this time.'

He pulls the trigger on the laser blaster once more.

If you think the Doctor should use his sonic screwdriver to save himself, go to 71.

If you think he should just run for it, go to 111.

52

'I have . . . acquired some useful items during my time as an imports and exports operative,' Ravenwood explains as he and the Doctor run along the coastal path, heading away from the village and towards the night-grey shadow of the lighthouse perched at the end of the rocky path. Down on the beach lies a wrecked ship, washed up on the sand.

'By "acquired" I take it you mean stolen?'

'One of them is a Firekind solar pulse cannon,' Ravenwood goes on, ignoring the Doctor's comment. 'If we can somehow lure the Kraa'Kn back into the sea, I think I can use the lighthouse mirror to amplify the cannon's beam and heat the water past boiling point, thereby eliminating the problem.'

'That's your plan?' the Doctor exclaims. 'Kill everything?'

'One way or another, we have to make sure this all ends,' the smuggler answers coldly.

Go to 53.

53

'Yes, one way or another,' the Doctor mutters. 'But I'm usually in favour of saving as many people as possible.'

'Which means sometimes having to make tough choices.'

'Don't talk to me about tough choices,' the Doctor growls, stepping close to the smuggler's face. 'Look, if we're going to do this, we do it my way or not at all – is that understood?'

'Of course, of course,' Ravenwood answers, holding up his hands in a gesture of defeat.

'Very well then. Let's get started.'

'This way,' says Ravenwood, with a gleam in his eye.

Reaching the lighthouse tower, the smuggler leads the Doctor inside and into a space littered with straw-filled crates containing everything from recycled spaceship parts to reclaimed thirty-eighth century teleport tech.

Climbing a rickety wooden staircase to the lantern room, the Doctor finds yet more curious technological devices that shouldn't exist on planet Earth, let alone in the eighteenth century.

'Okay, let's get to work,' he says.

Go to 133.

54

'Drink?' the barmaid asks as the Doctor approaches the bar.

'How did you guess?' the Time Lord replies.

'You look like you need one.'

The young woman opens the tap on a keg behind the counter and fills a pewter tankard with foaming brown ale. Placing the tankard on the bar, she leans forward and whispers, 'You've seen him too, haven't you? I can see it in your eyes.'

'I'm sorry. Seen who?'

'My poor love.' The barmaid's eyes fill with tears. 'At least, he was my love. When he was still alive.'

The Doctor stares at the girl, mouth agape. 'Undead Fred out there is your boyfriend?' he exclaims.

An awkward silence descends over the smoky room once again. A deep voice calls from a table, 'I think it's time you were on your way, stranger!'

Sensing it might be best to leave, the Doctor moves to exit the inn. On his way to the door he hesitates and, turning back to the barmaid, says, 'I'm sorry for your loss.'

Go to 45.

55

Sprinting for the wrecked ship, the Doctor throws himself through a great hole in the bow and presses himself behind a curving wall of wood, out of sight of the smuggler.

Hearing a sucking, slurping sound, he spins round and comes face-to-face with a horrifying vision – a creature that is half octopus and half man.

The monster moves towards the Doctor from the gloom of the hull, reaching for him with fingers like squirming slugs. Its skin glistens green-grey like that of some deep-sea-dwelling squid, and although its body is humanoid in form the horror's head has hundreds of writhing tentacles.

The Doctor can't help but give a cry of alarm.

'Kraa'Kn! Primitive, vicious and usually hungry!'

Then he is sprinting out of the wreck and back on to the beach in an effort to escape the clutches of the squid-man.

Go to 76.

56

Spinning about on his heel, the Doctor sprints across the rugged moorland, back towards his blue box.

Over the pounding of the double pulse in his ears, he hears the sound of a firearm discharging and the horse whinnying, startled by the shot.

'Well, that escalated quickly,' the Doctor gasps as he runs. 'Even quicker than usual.'

With a cry of 'Yah!' the rider spurs his steed after the Doctor.

The gun fires again and this time the Doctor realises what was wrong with the sound of the shot the first time – what he heard was not the crack of igniting gunpowder, but something more like the whoosh of a firework. It sounded like an alien firearm.

A patch of grass to the Doctor's right bursts into flame as a zinging red bolt of focused energy hits it.

Then he catches sight of something else: another silhouette, darker than the night sky, against the horizon. It is a lone building with a light shining from a single window. It looks like an inn.

If you want the Doctor to change direction and head towards the building, go to 23.

If you want him to keep heading towards the TARDIS, go to 8.

'These people need our help,' Bess insists.

'And that's precisely what I plan on giving them,' the Doctor presses. 'But I can't do that here, and if you've any sense you'll come with me. Otherwise you're going to end up served to the Kraa'Kn as part of a very special dish: Calamari's Revenge!'

'Is this what you do?' the barmaid challenges him. 'Run away all the time?'

'Yes, and I'm very good at it,' admits the Doctor. 'It's why I'm still here. And this time running away is going to help me to save this village.'

'Well, I won't leave! Not now,' Bess tells him.

If you think the Doctor should keep trying to persuade Bess to go with him, go to 15.

If you think he should get moving before the squid-men catch them, go to 70.

58

Leaving Bess alone, guarding the strange device in the lighthouse lantern room, the Doctor hurries through the night to where his TARDIS stands waiting patiently on the moor. He boards the time machine and, his hands working the familiar controls, he dematerialises it, then rematerialises down on the beach beside the shipwreck.

'Now all I have to do is send out a sonic pulse that will draw the Kraa'Kn spawn to this spot, then pilot the TARDIS back to the lighthouse lantern room,' the Doctor says, outlining his plan aloud to help him to order his thoughts. 'Then I'll activate the miniaturisation ray I've cobbled together to shrink them down to a portable size and Bob's your uncle! I'll whisk them off to somewhere light years away!'

Then another thought strikes him.

'But what about the Kraa'Kn mother out there in the bay? What do I do about her?'

If you think the Doctor should deal with the Kraa'Kn spawn before tackling the brood-mother, go to 73.

If you think he should deal with them both at the same time, go to 99.

59

The Doctor blearily opens his eyes, blinking them into focus as he slowly becomes aware of his surroundings.

He is slouched against a wall in the corner of a well-lit chamber. Large barrels line the walls along with a number of wooden crates, some of which have straw spilling from them. There are no windows and the air smells damp, so the Doctor assumes that he is underground.

Fortunately his hands are untied and he does not appear to have suffered any lasting damage. He clearly hasn't regenerated either; running a hand over his face, he discovers that his attack eyebrows are still in place.

On the opposite side of the underground storeroom, a passageway leads away into darkness. Next to this stands a makeshift table fashioned from an old door placed across a pair of upended barrels. Standing in front of the table is a man dressed in a long cape, his black hair tied in a ponytail. He has his back to the Doctor.

If you think the Doctor should challenge the man, go to 41.

If you think he should remain silent and continue to observe the man, go to 28.

If you think he should try to sneak out of the chamber unseen, go to 9.

60

Leaving the zombies far behind, the Doctor runs towards the coastal road. Once he is back on the bumpy, rocky track, he sets off in the direction of the TARDIS, hoping he can circle round and avoid running into the undead again.

Go to 35.

61

Crossing the chamber in only a few strides, the Doctor punches the palm-reader with his fist. There is an electronic beep followed by a whirring hum and the hatch opens with a hiss of venting gases.

The atmosphere in the room beyond the metal door is very different from that in the brick-built antechamber. The Doctor can barely see anything through the murky green mist.

Suddenly he finds himself face-to-face with the occupant of the vessel he has inadvertently discovered; it appears to be partly reptilian, partly fish-like, partly humanoid and wholly alien in form.

'Terileptil!' the Doctor gasps.

If you think the Doctor should get out of there as fast as he can, go to 79.

If you think he should stand firm before the alien, go to 105.

62

For a moment the stranger says nothing, but simply keeps his steely gaze fixed on the Doctor. Then his shoulders sag, the tension appears to leave his body and – most importantly – he lowers the gun in his hand.

'You're not from round here, are you?' he says at last.

'And neither are you, judging by that little lot,' the Doctor replies, nodding at the junk strewn over the makeshift table. 'So why don't you tell me why you are here?'

'I pursued a Vortex-sensitive creature called the Kraa'Kn to Earth.'

'Pursued?'

'I had hoped to capture the Kraa'Kn spawn and return with them to the fifty-second century.'

'And what were you planning on doing with the spawn then?'

'Trading them,' the man says, avoiding the Doctor's gaze.

The Doctor scowls. 'Trading them? To whom? Disreputable

alien warlords, no doubt. Yes, that's right, I know what Kraa'Kn are,' the Doctor snaps, seeing surprise on the man's face. 'To be used as biological weapons in their bloodthirsty wars of conquest. Shock troops, probably.'

'Turns out there's rather more of them than I was expecting. I was constructing a sonic beacon to try to lure them away from the village and trap them somewhere –'

'But you're not having any luck,' the Doctor interrupts, eyeing the tangle of wires and beacon parts on the workbench.

'Well, now that you've heard my confession, will you help me?'

'I'm thinking about it. You can call me the Doctor, but what should I call you? Apart from "idiot" obviously.'

'Ravenwood.'

'Let me tell you something, Mr Idiot Ravenwood. Your little shenanigans have put an entire village at risk of being devoured by hungry sea monsters, so I'm not entirely sure you deserve my help.'

If you think the Doctor should help Ravenwood anyway, go to 92.

If you think he should refuse to help the man, go to 108.

63

The Doctor keeps walking towards the sea until he is forced by the incoming tide to stop. If he's going to go out any further, he needs to take off his shoes and socks and go for a paddle in the hissing waves.

He can see the churning more clearly now, a little way out in the water – a great frothing in the waves as if a huge shoal of fish has become agitated. Or possibly something much bigger . . .

Then the Doctor catches sight of something closer to land, just out past the point where the waves are breaking on the shore: the glistening dome of a head rising from the sea.

Upon seeing it, the Doctor is immediately transported a couple of hundred miles up the coast and a couple of hundred years into the future – although more millennia have passed in his own lifetime since he first witnessed the Sea Devils emerging from the sea. The feeling of cold dread that fills his hearts now is much the same sensation as he felt then; he knows by instinct that the people who live in this place, at this time, are in danger and need warning.

The question is, what is the best way for him to alert them to this threat from the ocean's depths?

If you think he should run to the village, go to 76.

If you think he should head for the lighthouse, go to 131.

64

As the Doctor hurries into the night, a short tower becomes visible against the backdrop of the darkened moors. Soon he can make out the entirety of the church, as well as the low stone wall that surrounds an old graveyard filled with crumbling headstones and overgrown with weeds.

Not knowing whether the hanged-man zombie – or the rider, for that matter – is still following him, the Doctor thinks the best course of action might be to take shelter somewhere and work out where to go from there.

Passing through a gate in the graveyard wall, the Doctor is now on holy ground. *Well*, he thinks to himself, *it worked with the Haemovores. Sort of.*

If you think the Doctor should now hide behind one of the headstones in the graveyard, go to 132.

If you think he should seek sanctuary inside the church, go to 144.

If you think he should stay at the entrance to the graveyard since he is standing on holy ground, go to 93.

65

'No, I'll go,' says the Time Lord. 'I don't trust you.'

The sonic beacon feels heavy in the Doctor's arms as he jogs down the rough track from the lighthouse to the beach. Reaching the wreck, he places the beacon deep inside the shattered hull and switches it on.

As he leaves through the hole in the ship's side, he can already see figures approaching from the village and emerging from the sea – figures that are roughly humanoid, only with the twisting tentacles of octopuses for heads. Before long, the squid-men are piling into the cargo hold of the wreck, drawn as if mesmerised by the pulsing call of the beacon.

Not wanting to hang around and run into the squid-men, the Doctor starts to scramble back up the track, intent on reaching the TARDIS as quickly as he can.

The night is suddenly banished as a false dawn rises over the bay. The Doctor turns to see a beam of orange energy tear from the top of the lighthouse and strike the ship. The broken masts, tattered sails and splintered hull burst into flames, despite being soaked with seawater, trapping the Kraa'Kn spawn in the heart of the blazing inferno.

'Ravenwood!' the Doctor bellows to the heavens, venting his fury at the storm-racked sky.

Go to 83.

66

Moving with sinister determination towards the Doctor is a frock-coated figure that wouldn't look out of place at the Palace of Versailles, apart from its cracked porcelain mask and corroded finger blades.

'Well, it's been a while,' the Doctor says, a half smile on his face. 'What are you doing here?'

The clockwork robot says nothing and continues its advance, its mechanical steps accompanied by a remorseless ticking.

'You know, I ran into some friends of yours in London about a hundred years from now. They didn't have your dress sense or your flair, though. Same logical and relentless approach to harvesting human body parts to repair their broken tech, mind. Pathological, you might say.'

Tick-tick-tick goes the robot as it closes the distance between itself and the Doctor.

'Let's see if we can't piece this puzzle together,' the Doctor goes on, thinking out loud. 'Smugglers' tunnels full of technology that clearly isn't eighteenth century, or even terrestrial for that matter. A clockwork robot I last saw at the Court of Louis XV. I'd say you're just as much a piece of anachronistic contraband as that Fengarian laser blaster.'

The robot comes to an abrupt stop and tilts its head to one side as it regards the Time Lord with bird-like curiosity.

'I can hear the cogs turning.' The Doctor laughs. 'Good to know you're thinking things over. So, while you're in a thoughtful frame of mind, how about working out who's most likely to be able to get you out of here and back where you belong?'

With a grinding of gears, the robot suddenly activates again, lunging for the Doctor and seizing him in a vice-like grip.

'There's never a can of multi-grade anti-oil to hand when you need one, is there?' the Doctor says, lamenting his fate – a fate that there is no escaping now.

He blacks out.

Go to 59.

67

Bess and the Doctor head off along the clifftop path at a jog. The lighthouse looms before them, a grey shadow against the deep blue of the thousand-acre sky.

As they run, they get a panoramic view of the cove below.

'Dead Man's Bay,' Bess says, looking down at the beach with a wrecked ship washed up on it.

Out beyond the ship they can see a great commotion in the ocean, the sea seething with white foam. As they watch, a long, snaking tentacle emerges from the froth and thrashes about.

'What's that?' Bess gasps, breathless with shock and from having to hurry through the night after the Doctor.

'A Kraa'Kn brood-mother would be my guess,' the Time Lord replies. On seeing Bess's startled expression he adds, 'It's a Vortex-sensitive squid-like creature and its spawn are favoured by disreputable alien warlords, who use them as biological weapons and shock troops in their bloodthirsty wars of conquest.'

'It's a giant squid?'

'Yeah, go with that.'

Go to 134.

68

'I could come with you,' Bess says later, standing with the Doctor outside the TARDIS at the foot of the lighthouse.

A new day is dawning over the Cornish coast. The storm clouds are gone, chased away with the night by the rising sun, which casts its golden gleam over the beach and the smouldering charcoal-black remains of the ship.

'No, that wouldn't be right,' replies the Doctor, gazing deep into her eyes, a mournful expression on his face. 'You're far too ruthless.'

'Then you could temper my ruthlessness. Make me better.'

The Doctor laughs at that. 'What a preposterous proposition! No, that wouldn't work at all.'

'Why not?' the young woman persists.

'Because I'm already ruthless enough. I need a companion who keeps me on the level, keeps me grounded. With you by my side, who knows what kind of hell we might unleash.'

For a moment neither of them says anything. In the end it is Bess who breaks the awkward silence.

'I don't regret what I did. Not for a second,' she says.

'Oh, well, good for you,' growls the Doctor. 'Because I will regret it for the rest of my unnaturally long life. So you can have that on your conscience instead.'

With that, the Doctor steps inside the TARDIS, shutting the door firmly behind him.

A moment later a wheezing noise fills the air and, with its roof lamp pulsing on and off, the impossible blue box dissolves and vanishes, leaving the barmaid alone. She gazes out across the bay at the village of Bosmouth, her future still unwritten.

THE END

69

'How come the lighthouse is unlit, and on such a blustery night as this?' the Doctor asks the barmaid.

'Ah, well, the place has been abandoned for some time,' she says. 'Talk of ghosts and walking corpses. No one'll dare go there now.'

If you think the Doctor should ask the young woman about the mysterious rider, go to 47.

If you think he should ask her about the gallows, go to 89.

If you think he should talk to someone else, go to 109.

If you think he should leave the inn, go to 107.

'Suit yourself,' the Doctor says as he marches off up the slipway, adding under his breath, 'I ask you. Planet of the Pudding Brains!'

The crack of a pistol makes him start, in part because it doesn't sound anything like a flintlock pistol, which would be appropriate to the era; instead it sounds more like something he has encountered on a thousand battlefields across a thousand alien worlds.

The Doctor turns as a figure detaches itself from the shadows congregated around a narrow alleyway. It is a man in long leather riding boots, a cape about his shoulders, his sleek black hair tied back in a ponytail behind his head.

If the name Ravenwood means anything to the Doctor, go to 95.

If not, go to 33.

The Doctor activates the sonic, setting it to disrupt the power flow through the laser blaster.

The weapon sparks and crackles in the smuggler's hand, but it doesn't discharge. The man looks at the Doctor in frustration but his expression can't compare in intensity to the Doctor's glowering eyebrows.

'Now,' the Doctor says, not taking his eyes off the smuggler, 'why don't we try that again?'

The man is silent for several painful seconds before replying, 'Very well.'

If you think the Doctor should ask, 'Who are you?' go to 21.

If you think he should ask, 'Why are you here?' go to 62.

Managing to escape the grasping talons of the groaning zombie, the Doctor makes for the dark wooden door of the church. As he does so, a dreadful thought strikes him.

What if there are more of those zombies in the church? he wonders. Perhaps that's what's become of the local populace . . .

If you think the Doctor should enter the church and boldly face whatever lies within, go to 144.

If you think he should hide among the headstones from the shambling zombie, go to 132.

73

'Sonic pulse activated!' the Doctor announces, and the light on top of the TARDIS starts to throb in time to the echoing chime now being emitted by the blue box.

From where he is standing at the open door of the time machine, the Doctor peers out into the night. He can see figures approaching from the village and emerging out of the sea. The figures rising out of the water are roughly human-shaped, but with the slimy bodies and twisting tentacles of octopuses planted on their necks – there's no question that they are of the vicious alien species, the Kraa'Kn.

'Right, now to get back to the lighthouse,' the Doctor says, stepping back inside the TARDIS.

A few moments later, accompanied by its familiar wheezing noise, the blue box promptly fades into nothingness.

Go to 141.

74

The two agree to meet again out in front of the lighthouse, before going their separate ways.

Ravenwood heads for the beach, clutching the limpet-like sonic beacon in his arms, as the Doctor takes off once more across the moors. Running through the night, it is as if his feet somehow know of their own accord where to take him: straight towards the TARDIS.

The question is, though, should the Doctor stick to the well-worn coastal path to get there or trust his instincts to lead him safely through the pitch-black darkness of the moors?

If you think the Doctor should keep to the path, go to 106.

If you think he should take a more direct route straight across the moors, go to 94.

75

The Doctor has a sense that something isn't right – a sense developed over more than two thousand years of adventuring across all of time and space.

He retreats slowly across the moor and crouches down behind a patch of long grass. The rider doesn't even have a lantern, so he'll never be able to pick out the time traveller in the darkness. Now that the sun has set, it is almost pitch black on the moors, the moon hidden behind racing clouds.

Still in sight of his precious TARDIS, the Doctor watches as the rider reins his horse in before the strange blue box. Dismounting, the rider sets about examining the time machine and even tries the door.

If you think the Doctor should reveal himself and approach the stranger, go to 87.

If you think the Doctor should stay where he is and see what the stranger does next, go to 101.

76

Out beyond the breakers, the Doctor can see a dozen or more glistening figures emerging from the sea, their humanoid bodies mounted with octopus-like heads, a fringe of suckered tentacles writhing around beak-like mouths, their hands both webbed and clawed. They look like something out of a fisherman's worst nightmare.

'Surely you're the worst this night has to throw at me,' the Doctor gasps as he runs along the beach, heading for the village.

Out beyond the emerging squid-men, a tentacle as thick as a tree trunk uncoils from the sea, followed by another, and another.

'Me and my big mouth!' the Doctor groans. 'A Kraa'Kn brood-mother!'

Go to 139.

77

The Doctor whips out the wallet containing the psychic paper and brandishes it in the man's face.

But, before he can come up with some likely excuse for his being there, the man exclaims, 'You're a Time Agent working for the Shadow Proclamation? Well, you're not taking me in – dead or alive!' And, with that, he takes aim and fires.

A beam streaks past the Doctor's shoulder, exploding a chunk of brick in the tunnel wall.

'Steady on!' the Doctor shouts.

'Focusing crystal must be out of alignment,' the man mutters to himself, and then he says to the Doctor, 'but I won't miss this time.'

He depresses the trigger on the laser blaster once more.

If you think the Doctor should use his sonic screwdriver to save himself, go to 71.

If you think he should just run for it, go to 113.

Sprinting down the zigzagging tunnel, the Doctor reaches the spiral stone staircase once more. He takes the steps two at a time and is soon standing in front of the narrow door that leads back into the abandoned church.

He takes a moment to listen at the door, straining to detect any sound that might be coming from the other side over the pounding of the double pulse in his ears.

'Well, here goes nothing,' he says and, flinging open the door, he bursts back into the church.

If the Doctor has already visited the Hispaniola Inn, go to 142.

If not, go to 103.

Running from the antechamber past the rider, the Doctor follows the twists and turns of the passageway beyond until he finds himself in a tunnel that has been chiselled through bedrock and follows an ever-steepening incline.

Old smugglers' tunnel, he thinks. *If I follow it downhill, I will surely reach the sea, eventually.*

He's right, of course: the tunnel eventually brings him to the vaulted space of a sea-shaped coastal cave. And the tide is in.

The Doctor's olfactory senses are assailed by the stink of rotting fish and drowned seagulls. The only way out, other than back the way he came, is to follow a slippery ledge to the cave's entrance and, from there, climb the wave-lashed rocks to the relative safety of the cliffs above.

But as the Doctor is shuffling along the ledge, keeping his back tight to the wall, something rises from the dark and churning waters of the inlet.

First to appear is a host of writhing, grasping tentacles, then comes a snapping beak, as a Kraken rises from the depths in search of prey.

'This wasn't part of the plan,' the Doctor gasps, 'ending up as a menu item at the Calamari's Revenge! Let me guess –' he activates his sonic screwdriver – 'genetic mutation caused by exposure to non-terrestrial chemicals leaking from the fuel cells of the Terileptil ship buried under the church.'

A shrill whine fills the sea cave and the monstrous squid gives a screech of pain – the screwdriver's sonic emissions are working on its highly sensitive auditory chambers.

Unable to bear the pain any longer, the Kraken sinks below the waves again, leaving the Doctor free to complete his escape from the cave.

Safely making his way to the foot of the cliffs, his attention is drawn to a pulsing light at the top of the previously

dark lighthouse.

Go to 49.

80

Running down a cobbled street, the Doctor turns a corner in time to see two of the amphibious squid-creatures advancing on a young woman. She is trapped, backed up against the wall of a house and unable to escape them.

'Oi! Get away from her!' the Doctor shouts.

The creatures turn and, seeing the Time Lord through their inky-black eyes, start to move towards him, their tentacles writhing in the air.

The Doctor activates his sonic screwdriver and immediately a painfully shrill noise fills the air. The girl throws her hands over her ears in agony, but the effect on the squid-men is much more extreme. The creatures' tentacles writhe even more furiously and the Kraa'Kn turn and flee, sliding down the slipway and back into the sea.

'Thank you!' the girl gasps as the Doctor deactivates the screwdriver. He recognises her as the barmaid from the inn.

'It's what I do,' he says.

'I beg your pardon, sir?'

'I'm always saving people. I'm the Doctor, by the way.'

'And I'm Bess,' she says.

'You'd best stick with me, Bess – if you want to live, that is.'

Go to 67.

81

'I recognise that voice!' the Doctor declares, taking off down a cobbled street.

'Voice?' Ravenwood queries, chasing after the Time Lord.

Turning a corner, the Doctor sees two amphibious squid-men – the hideous spawn of the vicious alien species, the Kraa'Kn – advancing on a young woman who is backed up against a wall and unable to escape. For a moment he thinks it's Clara, until she drops her hands from before her face and he sees that it is Bess, the barmaid from the Hispaniola Inn.

'Get away from her!' the Doctor roars.

The creatures turn and, seeing the Doctor through their inky eyes, start to move towards him instead, clawed hands reaching out, writhing tentacles feeling the air for any tiny changes in pressure that might indicate movements they can't see in the darkness.

An all-too-familiar crack echoes from the close-packed

buildings and one of the squid-men drops to the cobbles, twitches, then is still.

'I said no more killing!' the Doctor yells, turning angry eyes – and eyebrows – on the smuggler, but he's too late to stop Ravenwood from firing his weapon again and dropping the second squid-man.

'Thank you!' Bess gasps.

'Don't mention it.' Ravenwood smiles.

'You are a liability!' the Time Lord barks, pointing an accusing finger at the smuggler.

'Ravenwood,' the other man says, ignoring the Doctor and offering the young woman his hand.

'Bess,' she replies, blushing.

'Now that everybody knows everybody,' the Time Lord says testily, 'and if we're quite done here, can we get back to the matter in hand?'

Go to 129.

'How did you manage to get your hands on all this stuff?' the Doctor demands.

'I . . . brought it here,' the man answers hesitantly. 'By ship.'

'Not by any ship an eighteenth-century Cornishman would recognise, I'll bet,' the Doctor mutters. 'I'd say you're a smuggler. You're even dressed for the part. Who are you really, and why are you here?'

'No, my turn,' snaps the man. 'What are you doing here?'

'Would you believe me if I said I was on holiday?' hazards the Doctor.

'You're not following me then?'

'Don't flatter yourself,' the Doctor laughs. 'You've asked two questions now, so it's my turn again.'

If you think the Doctor should ask once more,

'Who are you?' go to 21.

If you think he should ask, 'Why are you here?' go to 62.

83

'I sorted the problem, didn't I?' Ravenwood says later, without even the slightest hint of remorse in his voice.

'But it was not how I would have resolved the situation,' the Doctor replies, picking his words carefully. Standing at the door to the TARDIS, he looks to the eastern horizon, where a new day is dawning over the rooftops of the village of Bosmouth and the becalmed waters of Dead Man's Bay.

'We should join forces, you and I,' the smuggler suggests.

'Are you serious?' The Doctor laughs mirthlessly.

'Why not? Just think of what we could do. "Ravenwood and the Doctor – Galactic Exterminators." It's got a certain ring to it, hasn't it?'

'And that is why we will never work together. It is also why I never want to see you again,' the Doctor says coldly. 'If you know what's good for you, you'll go and hide under a rock somewhere, for a very long time.'

The Cornish coast is safe at last, but at the price of an entire species.

The Doctor doesn't wish the smuggler farewell. He simply steps inside the impossible blue box and closes the door behind him.

A moment later a wheezing noise fills the air and the TARDIS dematerialises, on its way to who knows where.

THE END

84

There are two tables that particularly capture the Doctor's interest.

At a long table in the middle of the room, a group of gruff-looking men sit and eye the Doctor suspiciously. They all puff on clay pipes, smoke curling from their nostrils up into the air.

Sitting alone in a nook beside a large fireplace is an old man. He has the build of a scarecrow and is muttering into his tankard of ale, or whatever it is he's drinking.

If you think the Doctor should talk to the young woman behind the bar, go to 54.

If you want him to join the group of men at their table, go to 104.

If you think he should talk to the old man sitting by the fire, go to 124.

85

'Well, this really is a surprise,' the Doctor says. 'I don't suppose you know what's going on around here, do you? Zombies and mysterious strangers with the wrong weaponry for this century aren't exactly normal, are they ? I mean, they are if you're me, but not for everyone else.'

The shambling corpse gives a horrid moan in reply, and a foul stench escapes its gaping mouth.

'All right then – well, actually, you're clearly not all right. You're undead, after all!'

If you think the Doctor should try to run for the safety of the church, go to 72.

If you think he should activate his sonic screwdriver and scan the corpse of the hanged man, go to 125.

86

Passing through a gate in the wall, the Doctor casts an unimpressed eye over the unkempt graveyard with its crumbling headstones, brambles and thick patches of nettles.

'Seems like there's precious little respect for the dead here,' he mutters to himself, then he looks to the church. 'Whole place abandoned. Maybe the local congregation is too busy worshipping elsewhere.' He turns his gaze to the coaching inn at the top of the hill.

Just as the Doctor is wondering whether to enter the darkened church or head for the inn, he hears shuffling footsteps and a moan, which he at first mistakes for the wind.

Then, out of the concealing darkness, he sees them come.

Skin rotten, grey faces, hair and teeth mostly missing – men and women long dead, judging by the state of them. Their hands are little more than bony claws stretching out towards the Doctor.

'Zombies.' He sighs.

The shambling forms of the undead are all around him now, encircling him, trapping him at their centre.

'Excuse me!' he says, addressing the zombies. 'Can one of you point me in the direction of the nefarious character who has doubtless enslaved you to her, his or its – delete as applicable – implacable will?'

'That would be me,' comes a voice from the darkness beyond the ring of decomposing bodies.

Then the zombies' filthy hands are on the Doctor, nails clogged with grave-dirt clawing at his clothes. He realises there is no escaping his fate.

He feels a sharp blow to the back of the head, and then nothing more.

Go to 59.

'Hello!' the Doctor calls, flicking back the flaps of his jacket and shoving his hands into his trouser pockets as he strolls nonchalantly out of the gloom and back in the direction of the TARDIS.

The rider looks round in surprise, eyes glinting beneath the brim of his hat, and his hand goes for the flintlock pistol holstered at his belt.

'She's an interesting piece, isn't she?' the Doctor continues, ignoring the firearm. 'One of a kind, you might say.'

'An antique,' replies the rider, keeping both his gaze and his pistol trained on the Doctor. 'Do you have a name, sir?'

'I'm the Doctor,' says the Doctor, holding out a hand and taking a step towards the man.

'Stay back!' the rider suddenly barks and fires his weapon.

Rather than the crack of igniting gunpowder, though, the gun's discharge sounds more like the whoosh of a firework.

A patch of grass at the Doctor's feet bursts into flame as it is hit by a zinging red bolt of focused light energy.

'Now, now, there's no need for that,' the Doctor says, clearly taken by surprise.

'The next shot won't miss,' growls the rider.

Not wanting to find out how true the man's sinister boast may be, the Doctor hares off across the rugged moorland towards the TARDIS. Then he catches sight of something else: a silhouette even darker than the night sky against the horizon. It is a lone building of some kind, with a light shining from a single window.

If you want the Doctor to head towards the building, go to 23.

If you want him to keep heading towards the TARDIS, go to 8.

88

'Argh!' the Doctor growls. 'It's *don't* press the big red button, isn't it? I should put a sign on it or something to stop me doing that.'

He picks up the phone, his fingers hovering over the keypad. 'I should call myself in the future to remind myself to do something about that. Or maybe I should call myself in the past so that I leave a note and don't do that in the first place. But then I already have done it, so I obviously didn't do that so . . . Oh, I give up!' He slams the phone down. 'That's a stupid idea. I'll just initiate the emergency landing protocol.'

The tolling of the Cloister Bell echoes throughout the endless corridors and chambers of the TARDIS.

'Don't you start!' the Doctor shouts to the air. 'I thought you were supposed to be on my side!'

The TARDIS lurches violently, throwing the Doctor across the console room. He lands hard against a handrail and staggers, before pulling himself upright.

'Did that just happen already?' he wonders aloud.

'Only I've got this terrible feeling of déjà vu.'

Go to 149.

89

'The gallows out on the road across the moors,' the Doctor asks, 'has it seen much use lately?'

The girl pauses. 'Too much,' she says, her voice breaking with emotion.

'Are you crying?' the Doctor asks in what is perhaps too harsh a tone.

'What if I am?' the barmaid says defensively. 'So would you if your one true love had been hanged for stealing!'

'Oh, I'm sorry to hear that,' the Doctor falters. He suddenly wishes he hadn't left his human-interaction cue cards in his other jacket, since the atmosphere is turning distinctly frosty. 'I'm sorry to have troubled you,' he says.

Then, not knowing what else to do, he heads towards the door.

Go to 107.

90

As the Doctor bounds across the nave, his footsteps ring from the flagstones, echoing in the eerie silence of the abandoned church. At this period in Earth's history, the church was at the heart of the local community – something bad must have happened for this place to have become deserted.

The latch on the narrow door rattles noisily when the Doctor touches it and he looks round in fear, worried it might attract further unwanted attention. However, upon opening the door, he is surprised to find a tight spiral stone staircase, which descends into the earth instead of rising to the tower. A glowing lantern sits in an alcove in the wall, making the shadows below even darker.

The Doctor is curious to know what is at the bottom of the staircase. Deciding that it's better to keep going forward, in case the zombie works out how to open the church door, he picks up the lantern and sets off down the stone steps.

At the bottom the Doctor finds himself at one end of a brick-lined tunnel. The air is thick with the smell of cold and damp. Holding the lantern aloft, he keeps moving.

Not much further on, the tunnel turns sharply by ninety degrees. In the wall to the right is a sturdy wooden door.

When he tries the handle, the Doctor discovers that it is locked.

If the Doctor has a large iron key, go to 100.

If not, go to 34.

91

'Who was that?' asks the Doctor, his wide eyes searching the night for the origin of the scream.

'We don't have time to find out!' cries Ravenwood. 'And it's not important, anyway – we have to deal with the Kraa'Kn!'

'Oh, really?' the Doctor shouts, angered. 'You're testing my patience, Ravenwood. Not in all my travels across time and space have I ever met anyone who isn't important to someone, even if that someone is only me.'

'If these people – all of them – are so important to you, then trust me, the best thing you can do is come with me.'

If you think the Doctor should focus on the bigger picture and go with Ravenwood, go to 52.

If you think he should ignore Ravenwood and follow the scream, go to 128.

92

'I'll help,' the Doctor says begrudgingly, 'but I'm not doing this for you. I'm doing it for all the innocent villagers – men, women and children. And I'll do it for the Kraa'Kn too. I'm sure they didn't ask to be pursued to Earth in the eighteenth century.'

He sighs, looking at the debris around them. 'First, we need to fix this luring beacon of yours.'

Thanks to the Doctor's engineering skills and the various tools Ravenwood has to hand, it doesn't take the Doctor long to accomplish what the smuggler had failed to do. They end up with a sonic device about the size of a pudding bowl that looks like an oversized metallic barnacle.

'Okay,' Ravenwood says, looking proudly at the completed beacon. 'Let's do this.'

Go to 112.

93

'Righty-ho!' the Doctor says, turning at the entrance to the graveyard to face the advancing horror. 'Come and have a go if you think you're hard enough!'

The shambling figure of the hanged man gives a ghastly moan and continues to approach.

'Now, are you sure you want to do this? I mean, aren't you worried you might burst into flame or crumble to dust the moment you cross this line?' The Doctor indicates the boundary wall of the churchyard.

The zombie keeps on coming.

The Doctor takes a wary step backwards.

The zombie stumbles up the step and through the gate and keeps on moving forward.

'Okay then. Plan B!' the Doctor announces.

If you think the Doctor should seek shelter inside the church,

go to 144.

If you think he would do better to escape through the graveyard

and make his way to the inn at the top of the hill, go to 132.

94

The moon suddenly breaks free of the clouds and the Doctor realises in horror that there is one major flaw in his plan: the way to the TARDIS is obstructed.

Advancing towards him across the moors is a pack of moaning zombies. The molecular fringe animation unit employed to bring life to the dead must still be active.

'Ravenwood!' the Doctor hisses under his breath.

Only one option lies open to him: he's going to have to double back to the road and hope he can circle round the undead that way.

The night is suddenly banished as light explodes over the bay. The Doctor turns to see a beam of energy tear from the lantern at the top of the lighthouse tower and strike the wrecked ship down in the bay.

The broken masts, tattered sails and splintered hull burst

into flame, and the Doctor hears the agonised squealing of the Kraa'Kn spawn caught within the blazing inferno – they had already been lured into a trap that Ravenwood had set for them before he activated the Firekind solar pulse cannon.

Go to 83.

95

'We meet again,' Ravenwood says, steel in his voice.

The Doctor engages full-on attack eyebrows in a furious scowl. 'Believe me, it wasn't intentional.'

'How can you be so sure?'

'Well, we didn't exchange phone numbers for a start. What makes you think I would want to see your annoyingly handsome face again?'

'What I mean is that it *was* my intention, Doctor,' Ravenwood replies. 'I have been watching you, following you.'

The Doctor eyes the smuggler suspiciously. 'Why?'

'Because I need your help.'

'Well, you're persistent. I'll give you that.'

'So, will you help me, Doctor?'

'No,' says the Time Lord firmly. 'But I will help the people of Bosmouth.'

'Then follow me,' says Ravenwood. 'We have to reach the lighthouse.'

'Very well,' agrees the Doctor. 'You lead the way.'

Go to 52.

96

As he descends a cobbled road towards the village of Bosmouth, the Doctor's gaze is drawn to a disturbance out in the harbour. A patch of sea is seething and foaming more furiously than he would have predicted, judging by the wind and the waves.

Then he sees something else: a light over by the lighthouse, but not at the top of the tower. It is a bobbing sphere, as might be cast by a lantern, moving along the rocky path towards the tall building.

'The game is afoot,' the Doctor mutters to himself.

If you think the Doctor should continue heading towards the village and the disturbance in the bay, go to 32.

If you think he should change tack and head for the lighthouse, go to 131.

97

Standing framed within the open hatch is a creature that is part reptile and part fish, although it is humanoid in form. Iridescent blue scales cover its body and its wide mouth is full of sharp, pike-like teeth.

'Terileptil!' the Doctor gasps.

'And who are you?' hisses the scaly creature before him.

'I am the Doctor!' the Time Lord declares proudly. 'And I've encountered your kind before. Not planning on attending any fireworks parties, I hope.'

'What is your purpose here?' gargles the Terileptil.

'My purpose? Well, I suppose that would be finding out what your purpose is here. I mean, I've met the welcoming committee and didn't find it very welcoming. You are a very long way from home, so why don't you come clean and tell me what you're up to?'

'What business is it of yours, Doctor?'

If you think the Doctor should respond with a thinly veiled

threat, go to 143.

If you want him to offer the creature aid, go to 29.

98

A faded sign hangs from a bracket above the inn door, swinging in the wind that whips over the moor. On it is a painting of an island, like something from a pirate's treasure map, and beneath that, in ornate lettering, the word 'Hispaniola'.

Pushing open the large oak door, the Doctor enters the inn. The door creaks shut behind him, blocking out the wail of the wind as silence descends over those sheltering inside.

The large, low-ceilinged room is filled with tobacco smoke, which makes the Doctor cough. Peering through the hazy air, he sees the bar itself on the far side of the room. Behind it a young woman with long, dark hair is serving drinks to the windswept customers.

The rest of the room is taken up with a jumble of chairs and tables occupied by all manner of individuals who have at least one thing in common: they have decided that sitting in here by the fire is far better than being out on the moors on a night like this.

'Evening, all!' the Doctor says, in an effort to ingratiate himself with the locals, all the while wishing he had someone here to guide him through this social minefield.

The inn's customers stare for a moment, before turning back to their pipes and pints. They talk among themselves, which the Doctor much prefers. But, then again, if the Doctor is going to find out more about this place and what's going on around here, he's going to need to speak to someone.

If you think the Doctor should walk up to the bar and order a drink first, go to 17.

If you think he should just talk to one of the locals, go to 109.

If you think he should simply leave, go to 107.

99

'I've got it!' the Doctor says in delight, peering out of the open door of the TARDIS at the waves crashing on the beach and the writhing tentacles emerging from the sea beyond. 'I mean, it's worked before. It's just a shame that I've only recently had the pool cleaned.'

With that, he darts back inside the TARDIS and activates the sonic pulse beacon. The lamp on top of the police box begins to pulse in time with the echoing chime now being emitted by the time machine.

Watching via the console monitor, the Doctor sees the Kraa'Kn spawn approaching from the village and emerging from the sea, making their way towards the TARDIS.

'Okay, here goes nothing!' The Doctor's fingers dance over the console controls.

Outside, accompanied by a whirring, wheezing noise, the blue box appears to phase in and out of existence, as the beach and the seascape beyond ripple and warp. It is as if they are being distorted by a heat-haze, or as if they suddenly exist in more than just four dimensions. At the same time, the Kraa'Kn fade into thin air, and the writhing tentacles out beyond the breakers disappear too.

Go to 150.

100

Fitting the key into the lock, the Doctor opens the door and steps through it.

He is surprised to find himself standing in a brightly lit chamber. All of the walls are constructed from crumbling brick, apart from the one the Doctor is now facing, which appears to be perfectly smooth metal. Set into this wall is a sealed hatch, and next to that a palm-reader. The light is coming from a group of crystals set into the ceiling.

'Vintaric crystals!' the Doctor exclaims in delight, recognising the illumination source.

On one side of the room he spots something that looks like a molecular fringe animation unit. 'And that is what's animating the dead,' he adds.

Standing on a hexagonal plinth on the other side is a strange vase-like container, apparently made of misted green glass.

'I recognise you too,' the Time Lord tells the vase. 'You're a soliton gas flask, aren't you?'

The Doctor starts, hearing the creaking of door hinges behind him. Turning, he sees a figure stoop to enter the chamber. It is the rider the Doctor saw out on the moors, his face hidden by the low brim of his hat.

Before the Doctor can say anything, the rider raises a hand and an intense purple beam shoots from his fingertips, striking the plinth.

'I'd be careful doing that in here,' the Doctor warns. 'Do you know how flammable soliton gas is when it's mixed freely with oxygen?'

The rider says nothing. He simply raises his hand, ready to fire again.

If you think the Doctor should use his sonic screwdriver to

block the beam emitter, go to 3.

If you think he should try to open the metal hatch and take

cover on the other side, go to 61.

101

'And what are you expecting to find?' the Doctor mutters to himself, intrigued rather than concerned, knowing that the TARDIS's Hostile Action Displacement System is active and operational. 'Most eighteenth-century Cornishmen I know wouldn't have the first idea what they were looking at right now. But then you're not most eighteenth-century Cornishmen, are you? That flintlock pistol tucked in your belt might look like it belongs around here, but the power cell set in the grip gives it away – I know an alien laser blaster in disguise when I see one.'

Having failed to gain entry to the blue box, the rider mounts his steed again, and – after casting a glance out across the moors, but without spotting the Doctor – sets off once more, over the blasted heath.

The Doctor considers the only signs of human habitation he can see from his spot: a church with a short tower, and a long building up on the crest of the hill. Considering the building's location and the era it is doubtless a coaching inn.

'So, where else do you go to find some adventure around here?' he asks out loud.

If you think the Doctor should head towards the church, go to 116.

If you think he should visit the coaching inn, go to 98.

If you think he should set off after the mysterious rider, go to 16.

Meeting the robot's advance, the Doctor grapples with the Terileptil's servant, the two of them crashing through the glass of the lantern chamber and on to the narrow wooden balcony beyond.

Their momentum is too great; the Time Lord and the android roll right off the edge of the balcony. The mechanical man plummets from the top of the tower, tumbling down the side of the cliff, and finally smashing to pieces on the jagged rocks at the edge of the sea.

The Doctor, meanwhile, is left dangling from the groaning balcony by one hand.

'Well, that didn't go quite according to plan,' he says, hauling himself back up on to the precarious platform, before stumbling back into the lantern room. The signalling device remains dormant.

'Now then,' he says, addressing the Terileptil once again.

'What I was going to say before I was so rudely interrupted

was, would you like a lift? My ship's parked down there –'

he points in the direction of the moor – 'and, if you like,

I can have you home centuries ago, as though you barely left.

What do you say? I've always wanted to visit Terileptus.'

THE END

103

Bursting through the door, the Doctor suddenly finds himself facing a pack of drooling zombies.

Despite their lumbering, unsteady steps, the dead quickly surround the Time Lord, and he finds himself trapped at the centre of a steadily closing group of clawing corpses.

'I don't suppose I could appeal to your better natures?' the Doctor says in a vain attempt at escape, but the zombies ignore him and continue with their relentless advance.

They reach for him, fingernails black with grave-dirt, and the Doctor knows that there is no escaping his fate . . .

THE END

104

'Gentlemen,' says the Doctor, sitting down at the table despite not actually having been invited to do so.

'Evening,' says a bald, broad-shouldered man with a thick black beard. 'Looks like we're in for another bad night.'

'Undoubtedly,' says the Doctor, not wanting to argue.

'Let's hope it's not as bad as two nights back,' chips in another, 'when that ship ran aground down at the bay.'

'Indeed not,' replies the broad-shouldered man, nodding. 'Storm was so bad it cleaned out the cargo and the crew, they say. Not one of them has been seen since.'

This is an interesting development, the Doctor thinks.

If the Doctor hasn't already talked to the old man sitting by himself but you think that he should, go to 124.

If he hasn't already had a chat with the barmaid but you think he should, go to 54.

If you think he should leave the inn, go to 45.

105

'And who are you?' hisses the scaly creature before him.

'I am the Doctor!' the Time Lord declares proudly. 'And I've encountered your kind before. Not planning on attending any fireworks parties, I hope.'

'What is your purpose here?' gargles the Terileptil.

'My purpose? Well, I suppose that would be finding out what your purpose is here. I mean, I've met the welcoming committee and didn't find it very welcoming. You are a very long way from home, so why don't you come clean and tell me what you're up to?'

'What business is it of yours, Doctor?'

If you think the Doctor should respond with a thinly veiled threat, go to 143.

If you think he should offer the creature aid, go to 29.

The Doctor makes his way along the path until he reaches the TARDIS at last. Flinging himself inside, he bounds over to the central console.

A moment later the blue box dematerialises, vanishing from the windswept moor and reappearing inside the cluttered room at the bottom of the lighthouse.

'You ready?' the Doctor shouts, sticking his head out through the TARDIS door.

'Ready!' the smuggler calls back, now having got himself in position at the top of the tower.

'Okay, let's do this!'

Back at the control console, the Doctor flicks a series of switches and, groaning, the time rotor starts to rise and fall with the regularity of a heartbeat. Suddenly a beam of intense blue energy shoots out of the light on top of the TARDIS and up the open stairwell of the tower, striking the vast lantern mirror above.

'Now!' the Doctor shouts, and Ravenwood activates the pulse cannon. The light is refocused by the cannon, which in turn emits a ray of golden flame as bright as the sun, banishing the night over the bay and turning it temporarily to day.

Ravenwood watches from the window of the lantern room as the squid-men stumble inside the wreck of the ship, drawn to the vessel by the sonic beacon he placed there.

Once they are all inside, the beam's waveform changes and it begins to pulse. With every pulse something incredible happens: the wreck and everything contained within it starts to shrink.

Soon it is no bigger than a jolly boat, and then, only a matter of moments later, Ravenwood can't even see it against the sand far below.

The Doctor steps out of the TARDIS to catch the smuggler

leaping down the stairs, taking them three or four at a time.

'Where are you going in such a hurry?' he asks, taken somewhat by surprise.

'Nowhere!' the smuggler calls back, disappearing through the door and into the darkness.

If you think the Doctor should go after Ravenwood, go to 115.

If you think he should relocate the TARDIS to the beach to collect the miniaturised vessel, go to 123.

Or, if you think the Doctor should rush back into the TARDIS and press a big red button on the console, go to 88.

107

'It's about as frosty out here as the welcome from the locals was in there,' the Doctor mutters to himself, now that he is outside the Hispaniola Inn again.

He pulls his red velvet jacket close about him in the bitterly cold wind, and considers where to go next.

If you think the Doctor should go and investigate the isolated moorland church, go to 127.

If you would prefer him to take a walk along the clifftop path towards the lighthouse, go to 148.

108

Putting the blaster down on the table, Ravenwood picks up something much larger. It's not a weapon the Doctor recognises, but its deadly purpose is plain.

'If you won't help me, Doctor,' the smuggler growls, 'then why do I even need to keep you around?'

There's no time for a quick quip or a timely put-down; there's only time to run. The Doctor makes a leap for the dark tunnel, a high-pitched whine telling him that the man's weapon is powering up to full charge. He hurls himself down the passageway just as Ravenwood discharges his weapon, and a chunk of wall explodes behind him in a shower of brick dust and crumbling mortar.

The Doctor doesn't dare look back, not once. He simply keeps on running. He doesn't even pause for breath when, in the darkness, he is forced to activate his sonic screwdriver, its soft blue glow helping him to see where he is going.

Go to 146.

109

Sitting at a long table in the middle of the room is a group of hard-bitten men who eye the Doctor suspiciously as they suck on the stems of their clay pipes.

Sitting in a corner by a large fireplace is a figure who is noticeably apart from the rest of the patrons. He is old, thin as a rake and muttering into his tankard of ale, or whatever it is he's drinking.

If the Doctor hasn't already joined the group of men at their table and you think he should do so now, go to 119.

If he hasn't already spoken to the old man sitting by himself and you think he should, go to 136.

If he hasn't already talked to the young woman behind the bar but you think he should, go to 17.

If you think it's time he left the inn, go to 107.

110

Moonlight shines through the high windows of the church, illuminating the memorials set into the floor between the flagstones. The same surnames feature again and again, giving the impression that only a few families have ever lived in the area or used the church to commemorate their dead.

Lost in his examination of the memorial stones, the Doctor jumps at the sound of wood scraping on stone. Unoiled hinges groan as the door opens, and the Time Lord spins round to see who has joined him within the holy building.

'You again.' He sighs, recognising the shambling gait and awkward posture. He has lingered too long and the zombie has found him again.

And, in fact, it is even worse than that.

Behind the zombie are more of its kind, moaning as if their last breaths are never-ending. There are at least twenty of them – men and women, young and old, all definitely dead.

Their eyes are sunken within nearly fleshless skulls, while thin strands of hair hang limply around their shoulders, skin peeling back to expose their insides. Their yellowing bones are visible in the sickly moonlight.

Seeing the Doctor – although the Time Lord's not quite sure how they can see anything through those ancient eyes – the zombies reach for him with hands like crooked, bony claws.

'Where's an angry, pitchfork-waving mob when you need one?' mutters the Doctor. 'Well, looks like I've outstayed my welcome. Time to exit stage right.' He looks towards the main door, which the zombies have conveniently left open. 'Or should that be stage left?' He glances at the door to the tower.

If you think the Doctor should head for the main entrance, go to 27.

If you think he should make a dash for the narrow door, go to 140.

111

The blaster fires once again, this time perfectly aimed at the Doctor's head . . . if the Doctor hadn't just thrown himself out of the way.

'What's wrong with a simple hello?' he gasps as he sprints out of the subterranean storeroom. But which way should he go?

If you think the Doctor should head back the way he came, go to 78.

If you think he should escape down the passageway that leads off the other side of the chamber, go to 121.

112

'Very well then,' agrees the Doctor. 'I'm trusting you, just this once. What's your plan?'

'Out there,' Ravenwood says, pointing at the storeroom wall but clearly meaning the coast beyond. 'The sea around Dead Man's Bay is now seething with Kraa'Kn spawn. It won't be long before they start coming ashore.'

'Kraa'Kn,' the Doctor growls. 'A primitive race so vicious that they'll fight on behalf of megalomaniacal warlords in some of the less well-policed regions of the universe. And if they've just spawned, they'll be hungry for their first meal!'

The smuggler looks down at the floor, clearly embarrassed.

'So what were you planning on doing once you'd finished fiddling with that sonic beacon of yours?'

'I was going to return to the lighthouse and put my plan into action.'

'Then what are we waiting for?' the Doctor exclaims.

Go to 52.

113

As the man discharges his weapon, the Doctor makes a leap for the dark, dank tunnel. He hurls himself down the passageway, a chunk of wall exploding behind him in a shower of brick dust and damp plaster.

He doesn't look back, not once; he just keeps on running, using the blue glow of his activated sonic screwdriver to help him to see in the darkness underground.

Go to 146.

DOCTOR WHO · CHOOSE THE FUTURE

114

Upon reaching the sandy shoreline the Doctor scans the bay for any sign of either the Terileptil or its android.

Then, high up on the rocky promontory that juts out into the storm-tossed waves, he sees a pulsing light atop the previously dark lighthouse.

The quickest way to the lighthouse is across the beach and past the shipwreck to a steep track that winds upward through the cliffs from a rocky inlet. As the Doctor is negotiating the slippery rocks at the track's sea-cave entrance, an ancient creature rises from the ocean.

'Let me guess – genetic mutation caused by exposure to non-terrestrial chemicals leaking from the fuel cells of the Terileptil ship buried under the church,' the Doctor says, staring at the churning waters below.

A host of writhing, grasping tentacles emerges, followed by a snapping beak, as the Kraken surfaces to claim its prey.

'Not so fast, Mr Tickle!' the Doctor shouts, whipping out his sonic screwdriver.

A shrill whine fills the air and the monstrous squid recoils in pain. The screwdriver's sonic emissions working on its sensitive auditory chambers, the Kraken disappears below the waves again, leaving the Doctor free to complete his climb up the cliffs.

Go to 49.

115

The Doctor chases after the smuggler, only to see the man mount his horse – which has somehow found its way to the lighthouse by itself – and take off towards the beach.

'Now what are you up to?' the Doctor wonders aloud.

Returning to the tower, he enters the TARDIS and activates the dematerialisation circuits.

A moment later the TARDIS rematerialises down on the beach. Opening the door, the Doctor steps out on to damp sand.

There in front of him, still in the saddle, is Ravenwood, and he is holding something in his hands. It is the miniaturised ship, containing its potentially lethal Kraa'Kn cargo.

'Thank you for this,' he says, smiling coldly at the Doctor. 'I really couldn't have done it without you. You win some, you lose some, eh?'

Before the Doctor can utter a word of protest, the man

calling himself Ravenwood kicks his heels into his horse's flanks and the animal takes off across the sand. They have not gone very far when the horse's eyes glow red, and rider, steed and a whole consignment of potentially devastating bio-weapons vanish into thin air.

'A cyborg steed with built-in Vortex manipulator. Well, that explains a lot, but you've not seen the last of me,' growls the Doctor, climbing back into the TARDIS and slamming the door closed behind him.

A wheezing noise fills the air. The TARDIS dematerialises, off to travel the tides of time in search of the smuggler and the Kraa'Kn.

You win some, you lose some indeed, and this time the Doctor has definitely ended up on the losing side. But he won't let it stay that way for long . . .

THE END

116

The Doctor hurries over the wind-whipped grass towards the church.

As he climbs the rise and approaches the short tower silhouetted ominously against the velvet-grey night sky, he sees the low stone wall that surrounds the church for the first time. Within its bounds is an overgrown graveyard filled with crumbling headstones, weeds, nettles and brambles.

He is about to pass through a gate in the wall when he hears the rustling of paper on the breeze and catches sight of a piece of pale parchment fluttering over the grass nearby.

If you think the Doctor should try to capture the piece of parchment, go to 43.

If you think he should ignore it, go to 130.

117

'Very well,' says the Doctor, sitting down opposite the old man.

'It's nice to have someone who's not from these parts to talk to,' his companion replies.

'How do you know I'm not local?'

'With an accent like that?' The old man gives a throaty chuckle. 'I'd wager you didn't come here by sea either.'

'I didn't, as it happens, but why would you say that?'

'That's another reason I know you're not from round here. If you were, you'd have heard about the Kraken. That thing is what wrecked the ship that ran aground a couple of nights back, I'm sure of it.'

The Doctor listens as the old man tells him all about the ship-sinking sea monster called the Kraken, and of the secret smugglers' tunnels that lie under the moors and link up with Dead Man's Bay, the natural harbour around which the village of Bosmouth lies.

Once the old seadog is done sharing his stories, the Doctor bids him farewell.

'Thank you for your time,' the Doctor says.

'Don't mention it,' the old man replies, returning to his drink.

If the Doctor hasn't already talked to the barmaid and you think he should do so now, go to 17.

If he hasn't talked to the group of men at their table and you think he should, go to 119.

If you think it's time he left the inn, go to 107.

Racing across the moors through the darkness, his feet seeming to know of their own accord where to take him, the Doctor heads for the TARDIS.

The moon suddenly breaks free of its shroud of clouds, and the Doctor realises in horror that his plan isn't going to work.

Advancing towards him across the moors is a pack of feral zombies. A molecular fringe animation unit, a piece of alien tech that can animate dead bodies, is clearly still at work here.

'Ravenwood!' the Doctor hisses under his breath.

With his way to the TARDIS cut off, the Time Lord is going to have to try something else.

If you think the Doctor should turn back, go to 60.

If you think he should head for the grim stone church, go to 11.

119

'Gentlemen,' the Doctor says, sitting down at the table despite not having been invited to do so by the party already occupying it.

'Evening,' says a bald, broad-shouldered man with a thick black beard.

'Nice weather we're having for the time of century – I mean year,' the Doctor hurriedly corrects himself.

'Aye!' The bearded man chuckles. 'So nice, in fact, that a cargo ship ran aground two nights back.'

'Is that so?'

'That it is. Mind you, whatever cargo it was carrying will have gone by now, washed out to sea. Isn't that right, lads?'

The man and his cronies burst out laughing, leaving the Doctor wondering just how much they really know about what happened to the ship and its cargo.

But what about its crew?

If the Doctor hasn't already spoken to the old man sitting by himself and you think he should do so now, go to 136.

If he hasn't already talked to the barmaid and you think he should, go to 17.

If you think he should leave the inn without further ado, go to 107.

120

The two men shake hands and, before the Time Lord can stop her, Bess throws her arms about him and gives him a huge hug. 'Goodbye, Doctor. And thank you.'

'Goodbye, Bess the barmaid,' he says, easing himself out of the embrace. 'And don't mention it.'

With a wave of his hand, the Doctor steps inside the TARDIS and closes the door behind him. A moment later, its light winking on and off, the blue box makes a wheezing noise and fades into thin air, leaving the smuggler and the barmaid alone on the beach, their futures as yet unwritten.

THE END

121

Sprinting past the villain with the laser blaster, the Doctor races off down the tunnel. He has no clue where it leads, but he is starting to get a pretty good idea.

'Old smugglers' tunnels under a church? One of them must lead to the sea,' he mumbles to himself. 'Otherwise how else would the freebooters get their gear in here without being seen?'

Sure enough, the rock-cut passageway starts to dip and the Doctor finds himself running down a steepening incline.

Ahead he can see the flickering light of another lantern, then something steps out of the darkness of the tunnel. The figure is silhouetted against the light source behind it, and the Doctor can make out the curls of a wig in a style favoured by the English upper classes during the seventeenth century. The figure moves with jerky steps, which are in turn accompanied by a steady clockwork ticking.

'No!' he gasps. 'It can't be!'

If you think the Doctor should charge past the

advancing figure, go to 36.

If you think he should stop and wait for the figure,

 go to 66.

122

'Hold on, you two,' the Doctor says into his walkie-talkie. 'Change of plan.'

It is a simple matter for the Doctor to link the molecular fringe animation unit to his sonic screwdriver so that he is able to access the control pod remotely. Leaving the subterranean storeroom, he makes his way back through the church, throwing open the door to the outside world only to find himself face-to-rotting-face with a horde of dishevelled dead.

'It's a mile to Bosmouth, I've got an army of the undead and a plan as cunning as a boxful of foxes. Hit it!'

Now that he is the psychic source the zombies have all latched on to, the Doctor only has to think a command and they will obey him. Directing his troops from behind, he marches them across the moors and down the road into the small fishing village of Bosmouth.

People start to scream in terror, thinking that they are under attack from a second nightmarish foe, until they witness the zombies engage the marauding squid-men in hand-to-hand combat, slowly but surely forcing the Kraa'Kn spawn across the beach and inside the wreck of the ship.

'Maybe these fishing folk will have more respect for the dead in future,' the Doctor mutters to himself.

The night is suddenly banished, as the light of a false sun explodes over the bay. The Doctor turns to see a beam of energy tear from the lantern at the top of the lighthouse tower and strike the ship down in the bay.

The broken masts, tattered sails and splintered hull all burst into flame, despite being sodden with seawater, and the Doctor hears the agonised squealing of the Kraa'Kn spawn caught within the blazing inferno.

Go to 83.

123

The Doctor opens the TARDIS door and steps out on to damp sand. Bending down, he picks up the tiny ship, making sure to keep all the miniaturised Kraa'Kn spawn contained within it.

Hearing the pounding of hooves on the beach, the Doctor looks up to see the smuggler charging towards him on his midnight-black steed.

'Whoa there, Quicksilver!' Ravenwood calls, as he reins his horse in and brings it to a rearing halt in front of the TARDIS.

'Looking for this, by any chance?' the Doctor asks casually.

'You caught me, Doctor,' the smuggler says with a bark of laughter. 'You win some, you lose some, I suppose.'

'I most definitely won this one,' the Doctor replies, steely-eyed and frowning.

'It's time I was on my way anyway,' Ravenwood says, seeing

the Doctor's hard look and turning his horse about.

'Yes, I agree. And what about all that alien tech you've left lying around the place?'

'I'm sure you'll be able to dispose of it safely,' the smuggler replies. With that, he kicks his heels into his horse's flanks and the animal takes off across the sand. It has not gone very far when its eyes glow red and the horse, and its rider, vanish into thin air.

'Oh, I see. A cyborg steed with built-in Vortex manipulator. Well, that explains a lot,' says the Doctor. 'Anyway, good riddance to bad rubbish.'

He steps inside the TARDIS and slams the door closed behind him.

A moment later a wheezing noise fills the air and the TARDIS dematerialises to go . . . who knows where?

THE END

124

'Hello!' the Doctor says, sitting down opposite the old man.

'Who's there?' the old man exclaims, looking up when he hears the Doctor's voice. 'Who is it?'

'Oh, sorry,' the Doctor says, meeting the old man's wandering gaze and realising that he must be blind. 'My mistake.'

'No mistake,' the man says quickly. 'Come, join me.'

'Very well,' replies the Doctor, staying put.

'It's nice to have someone who's not from these parts to talk to,' the old man says.

'How do you know I'm not local?' the Doctor asks.

'With an accent like that?' The old man gives a chuckle. 'I'd be willing to bet you didn't come here by sea, either.'

'No, I didn't, but how would you know that?'

'That's another reason I know you're not from round here. If you were, you'd have heard about the Kraken.'

'Local legend, I take it?'

'Not a legend. That monster's what took down the ship that ran aground a couple of nights back, I'm sure of it.'

The Doctor listens as the old man recounts the tale of a ship-sinking tentacled monster known as the Kraken, and tells of the secret smugglers' tunnels that lie under the moors and link up with Dead Man's Bay, the natural harbour around which the village of Bosmouth lies.

Once the old seadog has finished, the Doctor gets up to leave. 'Thank you for your time,' he says.

'Don't mention it,' the old man replies, returning to his drink.

If the Doctor hasn't already chatted with the barmaid and you think he should do so now, go to 54.

If he hasn't already talked to the group of men at their table and you think he should, go to 104.

If you think he should leave the inn, go to 45.

125

Retrieving the sonic screwdriver from his jacket pocket, the Doctor flicks it on. Keeping an eye on the advancing corpse of the hanged man, he analyses the data feed.

'Background radiation reflected from the rider through a cerebral impulse and transmitted to Undead Fred here, which creates an alternate energy pattern, which in turn stimulates the corpse at a molecular level, making it capable of autonomous physical movement. Or, in other words, molecular fringe animation!'

While the Doctor has been studying the sonic's read-out, the zombie has staggered closer. It lunges at him with a speed the Doctor would not have expected, and he finds himself in its steel-hard grip.

'This is all rather sudden, isn't it?' the Doctor says. 'I mean, we've only just met!'

The firework-like whooshing noise of a weapon discharging fills the air.

The Doctor tenses in agony as he is hit by a bolt of energy. Then he feels nothing else and slips into darkness.

Go to 59.

126

The Doctor blearily opens his eyes as he comes to and finds himself still at the entrance to the buried alien ship. Both the Terileptil and its android are gone, as is the soliton gas flask.

The molecular fringe animation unit remains, however; before he does anything else, the Doctor deactivates it. The alien and its android are going to be tricky enough to take care of, without an army of animated scarecrows or corpses on the loose as well.

He is certain now that the Terileptil is behind the disturbances that have been plaguing this area. What's more, the fact that the alien has abandoned its damaged craft suggests that its plans – whatever they may be – are about to come to fruition. But where?

If you think the Doctor should head for the bay, go to 114.

If you think he should make for the lighthouse, go to 49.

127

The Doctor strolls nonchalantly over the wind-whipped grass towards the church, his hands stuffed in his pockets, whistling to himself. The church is surrounded by an uncared-for graveyard – judging by the crumbling headstones and weed growth – which is surrounded by a low stone wall.

Passing through a gate in the boundary wall, the Doctor follows the path to the church door. As he puts his hand on the latch he hears shuffling steps behind him, and turns to find himself confronted by something out of a horror movie.

It looks like a man, but its flesh is grey and worm-eaten, its hair matted with black earth and almost all its teeth missing. The zombie's clothes are little more than filthy rags, while a frayed rope hangs loose about its neck – a noose, the Doctor realises.

Fortunately the church door is unlocked. Flinging it open, the Doctor runs inside and slams the door behind him, hearing the reassuring clatter of the iron latch falling into place.

It is eerily quiet inside the darkened church. Flicking on his sonic screwdriver, the Doctor makes his way cautiously through the gloom, the interior of the building now lit by the sonic's soft blue glow. He sees a door set into a curving wall on the far side of the nave.

'Must lead to the tower,' the Doctor murmurs, as if unwilling to impose on the eerie silence of the church. 'But what I need are clues – clues as to what might be going on out there on the moors.'

If you think the Doctor should study the interior of the church for clues, go to 110.

If you think he should investigate the narrow door on the other side of the nave, go to 90.

128

Running down a cobbled street, the Doctor turns a corner just in time to see two of the amphibious squid-men – alien Kraa'Kn spawn – advancing on a young woman who is backed up against a wall and unable to escape.

'Oi! Get away from her!' he shouts.

The creatures turn and start to move towards him instead, clawed hands reaching for him, writhing tentacles testing the air for any minuscule changes in pressure that might indicate the Time Lord's movements.

The Doctor activates one of his sonic's numerous settings and immediately a shrill, disharmonic whine fills the air.

The girl throws her hands over her ears, her face screwed up in agony, but the effect on the squid-men is even more extreme. The creatures' tentacles writhe furiously, and the Kraa'Kn turn and flee, sliding down the slipway back into the sea.

'Thank you!' the girl gasps, when the Doctor deactivates the screwdriver.

'Don't mention it,' says Ravenwood, appearing behind the Doctor. 'It was nothing.'

'For you maybe,' mutters the Time Lord.

'I'm Ravenwood.' The smuggler offers the young woman his hand.

'Bess,' she replies with a small smile, never once taking her eyes off his.

'And I'm the Doctor,' the Time Lord says testily. 'Not that anybody cares. Now, if we're quite done here, perhaps we could get back to the matter in hand?'

Go to 129.

129

'I'm coming with you,' says Bess.

'No,' the Doctor says firmly. 'It's too dangerous.'

'It's no more dangerous than staying here,' Ravenwood says, offering Bess a wink.

'He's got a point,' the young woman says, casting an anxious glance at the battle in full swing at the quayside.

'Fine, but on your head be it. I'm done with being responsible for people,' the Doctor grumbles.

'Are you sure about that, Doctor?' the smuggler goads.

'Shut up!' the Doctor snaps. 'Just shut up!'

He leads them away from the fighting, in the direction of the lighthouse.

Go to 147.

130

Something suddenly steps out from the gloom of the graveyard in front of the Doctor. At that same moment the clouds pass away from the rising moon, and the church and the graveyard are bathed in eerie light.

The figure standing before the Doctor is clad in filthy rags. Its flesh is grey and rotting, its hair matted with dirt, and its teeth nothing more than yellowed stumps. Most unsettling of all is the fact that a rope hangs slack about the zombie's neck – just like a noose.

'Whoa!' the Doctor exclaims, stumbling to a halt out of reach of the shambling corpse. 'I wasn't expecting to bump into a horror-movie extra in eighteenth-century Cornwall!'

Turn the page.

If you think the Doctor should try talking to the zombie, go to 85.

If you think he should sprint for the safety of the church, go to 72.

If you think he should make for the building on the crest of the hill, go to 2.

131

Moving as fast as he can, the Doctor makes his way to the clifftop path, and soon approaches the lighthouse. It is strange to see the tower unlit on such a night – strange and disconcerting. Why go to all the trouble and expense of constructing such an elaborate building to not make use of it?

The Doctor starts at the sound of a weapon – but it's more like a futuristic buzz than the crack of a pistol. As he turns, he sees a figure approaching out of the darkness. The man holds a curious pistol in his right hand, and he is pointing it at the Doctor.

'This is where it all ends,' the stranger declares.

If the name Ravenwood means anything to the Doctor, go to 53.

If not, go to 30.

132

As the Doctor darts between the carved crosses and subsiding headstones, shadowy shapes detach themselves from the impenetrable blackness between the tombs and advance towards him. The moon is revealed once more and the Doctor stifles a gasp, wishing that the clouds had stayed just where they were.

Approaching him is a crowd of creatures – men and women, young and old, all certainly dead. Bodies rotten, faces grey, hair hanging in clumps around their shoulders, shining bones visible through peeling skin in the chill moonlight. The zombies reach for the Doctor with hands that are withered, bony claws.

The shambling forms of the undead are all around the Doctor now, encircling him, trapping him at the centre of a steadily closing noose of corpses.

'Excuse me,' he says, addressing the zombies, 'but can

anyone point me in the direction of the nefarious character who has doubtless enslaved you to her, his or its – delete as applicable – implacable will?'

'That would be me,' comes a voice from the darkness beyond the ring of closing cadavers.

Then the filthy hands of the undead are upon the Doctor, nails black with grave-dirt clawing at his clothes. He knows that there is no escaping his fate now.

He feels a sharp blow to the back of the head, then nothing more as he blacks out.

Go to 59.

133

Making use of the Firekind solar pulse cannon he finds among the misplaced detritus, a Fengarian power cell and the guts of a Sontaran teleport unit, the Doctor cobbles together a bizarre contraption while the smuggler does what he can to help.

'It's finished,' says the Doctor at last, standing back to admire his handiwork.

'What does it do?' asks Ravenwood.

'Gets you, and the Kraa'Kn, out of hot water,' replies the Time Lord. 'Hopefully. Trouble is, we really need three people to put the plan into action. One of us needs to stay here to activate the solar pulse cannon, and one of us needs to direct operations from inside my TARDIS – and, seeing as I'm the only one with a key and the necessary know-how, that's going to have to be me. But, first of all, one of us is going to have to deploy that sonic beacon –' he points at an odd-looking device sitting on the floor in front of the lantern mirror – 'inside the shipwreck down on the beach, to draw the Kraa'Kn into it.'

'I'll do it,' offers Ravenwood.

If you think the Doctor should agree to let Ravenwood deploy the beacon before returning to activate the solar pulse cannon, go to 74.

If you think the Doctor should simply do it himself before returning to his TARDIS, go to 65.

134

When they reach the lighthouse, the Doctor discovers that the door at the base is unlocked. Pushing it open warily – the creak of its hinges horribly loud – he enters the darkness beyond.

The bottom of the tower is littered with straw-filled crates, which contain what the Doctor can only assume are spaceship parts, and other items of alien tech.

'I bet you weren't expecting that,' the Doctor says as he starts to climb the wooden stairs to the top of the abandoned tower.

Bess follows him up the precarious staircase. 'What are all those things?' she asks.

'Anachronisms.'

'Bless you.'

The top of the tower is the same as the base: cluttered with bits of curious machinery that shouldn't exist on planet Earth at all, let alone in the eighteenth century.

'I could use some of this,' the Doctor says, taking in a solar pulse cannon among the misplaced detritus.

'Look at this, Doctor,' Bess calls from the great glass windows of the lantern room.

If you think the Doctor, distracted by what's in front of him, should ignore Bess, go to 39.

If you think he should join her at the window, go to 18.

135

'We've met before, haven't we?' the Doctor challenges, remembering the mysterious rider he encountered galloping across the moors; so much has happened in the time since that it now feels like days ago. 'So who are you?' he asks.

'You can call me Ravenwood,' the man replies.

'I'm the Doctor.'

'Doctor who?'

'Just the Doctor. This is Bess, and you're right on time.'

'We need your help,' Bess says, turning imploring eyes on the man. 'Will you help us?'

'Well, seeing as half this stuff is mine –' the man indicates the alien items scattered about the lantern room – 'and seeing as that mess down there is also mine –' he points out of the window at the seething waters of the bay – 'and seeing as you asked so nicely –' he fixes his flinty eyes on Bess, a smile curling the corners of his mouth – 'how could I possibly refuse?'

Go to 147.

136

'Hello!' the Doctor says, taking a seat at the old man's table. 'Who's there?' the old man exclaims, looking up when he hears the Doctor's voice. 'Who is it?'

Only then does the Doctor see the man's clouded eyes and realise that he is completely blind. He won't have seen anything at all that's been going on around here.

'Oh. Sorry to trouble you,' the Doctor says and moves to leave.

'No trouble, young man,' the Cornishman replies, which brings a slight smile to the Doctor's mouth. 'You can join me, if you like.'

If you think the Doctor should stay and talk to the old man, go to 117.

If he hasn't already talked to the barmaid and you think he would be better off doing so, go to 17.

If he hasn't already spoken to the group of men at their table and you think he should, go to 119.

If you think he should leave the inn, go to 107.

137

As the Doctor runs to stop the Terileptil from activating the beacon, the android takes aim with its handgun and fires.

The blast misses the Doctor but strikes the lantern mirror, bouncing off it and hitting the alien device. There is an explosion of sparks and the device bursts into flames.

The force of the blast sends the Doctor reeling, and before he knows it he's tumbling backwards down the stairs, head over heels, all the way to the bottom.

It is then that a secondary explosion occurs, and the top of the lighthouse is consumed by an expanding ball of unleashed energy.

As shards of stone and charred, broken beams rain down around him, the Doctor picks himself up and flees. He is bruised and battered, but he is still alive, unlike the Terileptil. Plus, he is a Time Lord and more resilient than many other humanoid life forms.

There is nothing more to be done here. The Terileptil is dead, its android destroyed and the mystery that led the Doctor to this point solved.

It is time he was on his way again, for somewhere out there in the universe some other place in some other time has need of the Doctor.

THE END

138

'There's only enough charge for one attempt at this,' the Doctor says, considering the makeshift device before him. 'A flick of the switch and it'll all be over, one way or another . . . But do I have the right? To choose to let one species live over another?'

'What do you mean, Doctor?' asks Bess, confused. 'Who are you?'

'I've had that debate with myself before,' he says, in full flow now, 'and we all know how that ended. And what if this is the last brood-mother left in the universe? Do I eliminate an entire race just to save a few hundred people of a species that will go on to proliferate throughout the cosmos anyway?'

'If you can't make the hard choices, then I will,' Bess says, and there's a fire in her eyes. 'I'll do what needs to be done. It's an easy choice for me.'

'No!' bellows the Doctor, but he's too late. Bess flicks the switch.

Once activated, the device's simplistic controls mean that it can't be turned off; it will only stop once the fuel cell has run dry.

Go to 141.

139

Even as he runs through the village towards the ocean, the Doctor knows that he is too late.

The villagers are engaged in battle with Kraa'Kn spawn that have emerged from the foaming surf – alien horrors walking on two legs, partly humanoid and partly octopus-like. Captain Henry Avery of the *Fancy* himself would think twice before taking any of them on, even armed with his cutlass and no matter how much grog he had downed beforehand.

Ducking and diving between the battling villagers and their monstrous attackers, the Doctor helps where he can – catching a falling person here, giving a creeping Kraa'Kn a shove there – but he knows that he is merely prolonging the inevitable. He needs to try something else.

The crack of a pistol makes the Doctor start. It doesn't sound anything like a flintlock pistol, though; it sounds more like the kind of alien weaponry the Doctor has encountered on a thousand battlefields across a thousand alien worlds.

If you think the Doctor should turn and face whoever fired the weapon, go to 145.

If you think he should make a run for it, go to 131.

140

In a few swift bounds the Doctor is across the church and throwing open the narrow door. He races through it and slams it shut again behind him, wedging it closed with an old birch broom he finds propped in a corner.

Turning from the now hopefully secure door, the Doctor prepares to walk up a staircase to the top of the tower . . . but finds he is actually standing at the top of a spiral staircase that descends into the earth.

A lit lantern sits in an alcove and so, being curious, the Doctor picks it up and sets off down the stone steps into the unknown.

At the bottom of the stairs he finds himself at one end of a brick-lined tunnel. The air is thick with damp, and moisture glistens against the walls. Holding the lantern out before him, the Doctor keeps moving.

He has not travelled far when the tunnel turns sharply left.

In the wall to the right is a sturdy wooden door. When the Doctor tries the handle, he discovers that the door is locked.

If the Doctor has a large iron key, go to 100.

If not, go to 34.

141

The night is abruptly banished as the light of a false sun explodes over the bay. A spear of energy tears from the lantern room at the top of the lighthouse and strikes the ship down in the bay.

The broken masts, tattered sails and splintered hull all burst into flame, despite being sodden with seawater. The beam then tracks across the beach, turning the sand it touches to glass, until it hits the sea.

Without waiting for the Doctor, Bess has activated the solar cannon. The Time Lord had planned to use the weapon to create a makeshift miniaturisation ray, but since he hasn't had a chance to complete his adaptations it is still nothing more than an utterly lethal heat ray.

As the sea begins to boil, the agonised squealing of the creatures lurking beneath the waves carries over the howling wind. It is a sound that chills Bess to the very depths of her soul.

Go to 68.

The Doctor is surprised to find himself alone inside the church, but for a young woman standing at the open door. 'Who's there?' he shouts.

'It's me – Bess!' calls the woman, and the Doctor recognises her as the barmaid from the inn. She is wearing a long red dress made of sturdy material, and has a black woollen shawl pulled close about her shoulders against the cold.

'You need to get out of here,' the Doctor announces, grabbing her by the hand and running from the building.

'Why?'

'Zombies, laser-blaster wielding Cornishmen – take your pick.'

The chill wind whips through their hair as they run down from the church and across the moor, in the direction of the coast.

'Something's going on around here and I'm determined to find out what,' the Doctor declares. 'A little local knowledge always comes in handy, so what do you say, Bess the barmaid?

Where should we go now?'

'The village, to help the people there?' Bess offers. 'Or the lighthouse, for a better vantage point?'

If you think the Doctor and Bess should go to the village, go to 37.

If you think they should go to the lighthouse, go to 67.

143

'When I said I've encountered your kind before, what I really meant was I've stopped your kind before.'

'Why would you want to impede my plan to leave this world?' asks the alien.

'You don't want to turn the planet into a plague-ravaged wasteland, terraforming it for your species in the process?'

'That would not be practical,' explains the Terileptil. 'My craft crashed on this world. In its damaged state, the vessel's operating systems automatically activated the stasis protocols designed to keep the crew alive until help arrives.'

As the alien speaks, gill flaps on the side of its head open and close independently of its speech patterns as it inhales the soliton gas.

'But help did not come,' it continues. 'I remained here, trapped, for centuries. In the interim, a temple was raised atop the crash site, over the place where my ship lay buried.

I was only awakened from my stasis-sleep when the humans came, smugglers looking for somewhere to hide their wares.'

'So why the android disguised as one of the humans?' the Doctor asks, intrigued now.

A low hiss escapes from between the Terileptil's fish-like teeth. 'Why should I answer any more of your questions, Doctor, when you have already stated that all you plan to do is bring an end to my schemes?'

'Now hang on. I only said that because –'

The Doctor's protests are silenced when another bolt of purple energy pierces the murky atmosphere on board the Terileptil ship, striking him in the back.

The Doctor falls to the floor, unconscious.

Go to 126.

144

Fortunately the church door is unlocked. Flinging it open, the Doctor runs inside and slams it closed behind him, hearing the reassuring clatter of the iron latch as it catches.

It is eerily quiet inside the dark church. Flicking on his sonic screwdriver, the Doctor makes his way cautiously through the gloom, the interior of the building now lit by the sonic's soft blue glow. He spots a narrow door set into a curving wall on the far side of the nave.

'Must lead to the tower,' the Doctor whispers, as if wary of disturbing the stillness of the church. 'But what I need are clues – clues as to what might be going on out there on the moors.'

If you think the Doctor should study the interior of the church for clues, go to 110.

If you think he should investigate the narrow door on the other side of the nave, go to 90.

145

The Doctor turns as a figure detaches itself from the shadows around the entrance to a narrow alleyway. It is a man wearing knee-high leather riding boots and a cape, his long black hair tied in a ponytail behind his head.

If the name Ravenwood means anything to the Doctor, go to 95.

If not, go to 33.

The Doctor races off down the tunnel. He has no idea where it leads, but he is starting to have his suspicions.

Old smugglers' tunnel, he thinks. *Heading downhill, so it must eventually lead to the sea. Otherwise how else would smugglers get their goods to a storeroom without being seen?*

Sure enough, the brick-lined section of the tunnel soon becomes a passageway chiselled through the rock itself, which goes downhill more and more steeply. Eventually this passage gives way to the rugged shape of a cave, and the Doctor wrinkles his nose at the smell of rotting fish.

Broken barrels and boxes lie partially buried in the sand, along with coils of tarred rope and glass bottles half full of seawater.

His footsteps crunching on the cave's shingle floor, the Doctor emerges at last on to the shore, below towering grey cliffs.

Stumbling down the beach, he peers through the night, taking in the scene before him.

To his left he can see the twinkling lights of a village that hugs the cliffs surrounding a natural harbour. To his right is the looming silhouette of the lighthouse, while in front of him is the wreck of a ship.

Hearing the sound of footsteps from the cave, the Doctor turns slowly, hands half in the air, already knowing what he will see: the mysterious man from the smugglers' storeroom, who also happens to be a smuggler himself. More worrying, though, is the alien blaster held tight in both of the smuggler's hands.

'No more running,' the man says and takes aim.

If the Doctor has met Bess the barmaid, go to 13.

If not, go to 31.

'And this is all yours?' The Doctor looks around at the crates of futuristic tech on the floor of the lighthouse tower. He sounds unconvinced.

'Yes,' Ravenwood says, a cocky smile on his face.

'You acquired it all yourself – by wholly legal means?'

'Ask me no questions, Doctor –'

'And you'll tell me no lies. You'd better stop talking, then, hadn't you?'

The smuggler grins at Bess. 'Who among us hasn't bent the rules from time to time?'

'Well, there's bending and then there's smashing into tiny smithereens,' the Doctor scoffs.

'Like you do with the laws of time?'

'All right, that's enough out of you,' the Doctor says, pointing at Ravenwood. 'There's work to be done.'

About half an hour later, after a lot of frantic fiddling with the tech Ravenwood has stored in the abandoned lighthouse, the Doctor is ready to put his plan into action.

'Bess, you stay at the top of the tower. Clever Boy here is going to get down to the beach as fast as he can and hide that sonic beacon –' the Doctor points at the large limpet-shaped device in the smuggler's arms – 'somewhere deep inside the hull of that ship, and switch it on. Then, on my mark, you flick the switch on that solar pulse cannon.'

'The thing that looks like a big spyglass?' the barmaid asks uncertainly.

'Yes, the big spyglass thingy.'

'And where will you be, Doctor?' Ravenwood asks.

'I'll be in my TARDIS, putting the final piece of the puzzle in place. We'll keep in touch using these.'

He tosses the other two a walkie-talkie each.

'One of mine?' Ravenwood asks, looking uncertain.

'No, one of mine,' replies the Doctor. 'Remember, wait for my mark.'

Then he's off, sprinting back along the rough coastal road, heading for the TARDIS.

If you think the Doctor should stay on the road, go to 35.

If you think he should take the more direct route across the moor, go to 118.

148

The wind whipping through his grey hair, the Doctor makes his way back across the moor towards the rugged Cornish coastline.

Following a well-worn path, he soon rounds the headland and finds himself looking down at a broad bay. To the left he can see the twinkling lights of a village that hugs the cliffs, and a path descending to the sea. To his right is the unlit lighthouse, while below him the tide is going out, leaving behind it a vast expanse of dark, wet sand.

Out in the bay, a patch of sea seethes and foams more furiously than he would have predicted, judging by the wind and the waves.

But the thing that has attracted the Doctor's attention is the ship that appears to have run aground on the beach. With its three tall masts, it looks like a cargo ship, but one that has seen better days. Its sails are in tatters and the boat is listing to one side.

What could have caused it to come ashore like this, and what has become of its crew?

If you think the Doctor should scramble down to the bay, go to 32.

If you think he should make his way to the village, go to 96.

If you think he should visit the lighthouse, go to 131.

149

'We appear to be stuck in a time loop,' the Doctor says to himself, holding tight to the control console as the TARDIS is tossed about on the time tides like a message in a bottle.

He pulls a lever and the bucking stabilises a little.

'Come on, old girl, don't fail me now!' he says and punches a big red button in the middle of the console.

There is an almighty bang, and sparks rain down from somewhere in the vaulted dome of the console chamber.

Go to 88.

'So where are they, Doctor? The Kraken and its young?'

Bess asks later, standing with the Time Lord outside the

TARDIS at the foot of the lighthouse.

'In there,' he says, jerking a thumb at the police box.

'In there?'

'In the swimming pool, to be precise.'

'What's a swimming pool?' the barmaid asks, confused.

'That's not important. The important bit for you

to understand is that the TARDIS is dimensionally

transcendental. It's bigger on the inside.'

'Like a ship in a bottle, you mean?'

'Well, no . . . but, if it helps, you can think of it that way.'

A new day is dawning over the Cornish coast. The storm

clouds have gone, chased away with the night by the rising

sun, which casts its golden gleam over the beach and the

storm-lashed shipwreck.

'What happens now?' Bess asks.

'I'll find some quiet backwater world,' the Doctor says. 'A Level Three planet, or an ocean moon somewhere. And then I'll release the Kraa'Kn back into the wild.'

'No, I meant . . . what happens to me?' the young woman says, looking disheartened.

'Now you get on with your life, Bess the barmaid,' the Doctor replies, a kind smile playing about his lips. 'Move on. Go off somewhere on a brand-new adventure. Or settle down, raise a family. It's up to you. Just think, though – what a great story you'll have to tell your grandchildren now!'

'About the madman I met with a blue box?'

'About the night you saved the village of Bosmouth. The night of the Kraken!'

With that, the Doctor steps inside the TARDIS, shutting the door behind him. A moment later a wheezing noise fills the air and, with its roof lamp pulsing, the police box dissolves and vanishes, leaving the barmaid alone. She gazes out across the bay at the village of Bosmouth, her future still unwritten.

THE END

COMING SOON